THE
DRAGON
DETECTIVE
AGENCY
THE CASE OF THE
MISSING CATS

Gareth P. Jones

First published in Great Britain in 2006 by Bloomsbury Publishing Plc,
36 Soho Square, London, W1D 3QY

A CIP catalogue record of this book is available from the British Library

ISBN 978 0 7475 8641 8

Printed and bound in Great Britain by Clays Ltd, St Ives Plc

3 5 7 9 10 8 6 4 2

All papers used by Bloomsbury Publishing are natural, recyclable products made from
wood grown in well-managed forests. The manufacturing processes conform
to the environmental regulations of the country of origin.

To Lisa for discovering this story
and encouraging me to write it
– G.J.

Chapter One

Dirk Dilly reclined with his feet resting on his desk, watching the smoke curl up from his mouth and fill the room. It spiralled up and then, as it caught in a breeze coming from the window, swooped back down. Business was slow. If the truth be told, he wasn't sure how long he'd been sat there. Two hours? Three? He could turn his head to look at the clock but it all seemed like so much effort. Anyway, he had never quite got to grips with telling the time. It was such a peculiar method of measuring things. Sixty seconds in a minute. Sixty minutes in an hour. Twenty-four hours in a day. He understood the principle, all right. It just seemed like a funny way to chop up time.

Dirk listened to the traffic passing and closed his eyes. He felt so relaxed that when the phone rang, harshly breaking the trance he was in, he fell backwards, his long, scaly tail lashing out, knocking the clock clean off the wall. It smashed on the floor.

'Rats,' he growled with such force that a small thin line of fire darted from his mouth. The flames caught a pile of yellowing newspapers that Dirk hadn't got round to filing yet, setting them alight.

'Big rats,' he said, springing to his feet. He threw the contents of his glass of neat orange squash at the spreading fire. It was woefully inadequate. The fire reached the curtains. Dirk looked around in panic. In the corner of the room was an old fire extinguisher. He whipped out his tail to grab it, but rather than grabbing it properly his tail caught the pull chord, immediately setting it off. White foam shot across the room and the fire extinguisher spun around, covering everything in sight. Everything, that was, except the fire, which was now blackening the ceiling.

'Big fat rats!'

There was only one thing for it. The painful option. He flapped his wings a couple of times, and lifted himself into the air. Then with a pre-emptive wince he threw himself against the curtains and ceiling. The whole building shook and Dirk landed heavily on his desk. He lifted his head and looked up. The fire was out. There was a moment's pause before the pain registered.

'Owwww!' he groaned.

His scaly, red back was fireproof, but he had landed with some force on his soft, green underbelly, which was now making an alarming ringing noise.

'I must have hurt myself pretty bad,' he muttered worriedly. 'What does a ringing belly mean?'

Tentatively he lifted himself up on his four legs to examine the damage. The ringing grew louder. He took a deep breath and looked down. To his great relief he found he had been lying on the telephone. He climbed off the desk and sat down behind it, catching his breath before answering.

'The Dragon Detective Agency. Dirk Dilly speaking.'

'Hello, are you a detective?'

It was a human child, a girl, by the pitch of the voice.

'How old are you?'

'Eleven. Why?'

'That's too young. Goodbye.'

Dirk put the phone down.

Kids, he thought. *Time wasters.*

And that was that.

Or rather that would have been that had the phone not started ringing again. In actual fact, that was going to be anything but that. By picking up the phone a second time he made sure that that was about as far from that as was humanly – or even dragonly – possible.

'Hello?' said the girl's voice again.

'What do you want, kid?' he said gruffly.

'My cat's been stolen.'

'I don't do animals.'

On the other end of the phone there came a strange gurgling, hiccuping, wailing, noise. She was crying.

'Listen,' said Dirk, a little softness creeping into his voice in spite of himself.

But the noise kept coming.

'Listen,' he said more sternly.

The girl still sobbed.

'All right, I'll find your cat.'

The crying stopped suddenly and the voice said with surprising brightness, 'Great. My address is forty-three Elliot Drive. The cat's name is Willow.'

'And have your parents looked for the cat?' he asked.

'I'm not even sure they know we have a cat,' she replied.

'Why do you think it's been stolen?'

'Because Willow always comes in when I call her, but she didn't tonight.'

'Tonight? When did you last see her?'

'This morning.'

'So she's been missing for how long?'

'I normally call her for tea at about four o'clock.'

Dirk glanced at the space on his wall where the clock should have been, then looked down to where it lay on the floor. He flipped it over with his tail. It had stopped with the big hand pointing at the six, and the smaller halfway between the four and the five. If he wasn't mistaken, it was half past four.

'You're telling me that your cat has been missing for thirty minutes and you've called me?'

'I told you. She always comes when I call her.'

'Hey, kiddo, I'm going to put the phone down. Don't ever phone me again. Don't even think about it. Don't even think about thinking it. If you even think about thinking about thinking about . . . Where was I?'

But the girl didn't answer. Instead the awful noise started again, growing louder and louder like an air-raid siren. Dirk wasn't exactly soft-hearted and he had no love of humans, let alone their small annoying offspring, but the noise was so horrible that he knew that even if he put the receiver down the memory of it would linger on. And so, against every molecule of common sense in his large, scaly body, he put the phone back to his long pointy ear and said, 'All right. I'll check it out.'

'Great,' said the girl cheerfully. 'My name is Holly, by the way. Holly Bigsby.'

After getting the cat's description, Dirk put the phone down and prepared to leave. It wasn't his usual sort of work. Normally he trailed cheating husbands, found teenagers who had run away from home or took photos of people off work with bad backs that were taking trampolining holidays.

He slipped his notebook behind his wing and peeked though the slatted blinds that hung in front of the window. Satisfied that no one was looking, he pulled up the blinds and pushed open the window. What could be simpler than a missing cat? It was probably stuck up a tree or had found a woman next door with fuller-fat milk or maybe it had been run over. No, this would be an easy case. He spread his wings, flapped them a couple of times and leapt out.

Chapter Two

You may be wondering what a dragon was doing working in London as a private detective. The answer is that if you're going to be a private detective, London is a large city with lots of people with lots of problems, so there's plenty of work to be had.

The other advantage of London for your average jobbing dragon is that hardly anyone ever looks up, which means that even if you are a four-metre-long, red-backed, green-bellied, urban-based Mountain Dragon, as long as you stick to roofs no one's ever going to see you.

Of course, there had been some close calls. But even if someone did look up in the middle of

Piccadilly Circus and catch a glimpse of a medium-sized dragon leaping overhead, by the time they had blinked or rubbed their eyes or tapped their husband on the arm to say, 'Look, a medium-sized dragon just flew past,' by that time Dirk was safely out of sight.

And the husband would say something like, 'A dragon? In London? Don't be ridiculous.'

And his wife might reply, 'That's what I saw.'

And he would say, 'Maybe it floated over from China Town. They have big long dragons for Chinese New Year.'

And she would say, 'When is Chinese New Year?'

And so on until one of them would say something along the lines of, 'We haven't had Chinese takeaway for ages. Let's have one tonight. Mmmm . . . sweet-and-sour pork.' And the memory of seeing a dragon would vanish as quickly as the dragon had himself.

While having to remain unseen is a disadvantage for a teacher or a bank clerk or an insurance salesman, it is a positive advantage for a private detective. Dirk only ever spoke to clients over the phone. In fact, the only face-to-face interaction he ever had with humans was with his elderly landlady, Mrs Klingerflim, who lived below his office. Although she claimed to be able to see perfectly well through her thick glasses, she was clearly as blind as a bat. Dirk had discovered this when she walked into his office and caught him asleep, head slumped over his desk.

'Oh, I am so sorry,' she had said as she opened the door.

Dirk had awoken with a start. 'Er, Mrs Klingerflim. I . . . I can explain,' he had said, ducking behind the desk.

'No need, Mr Dilly. After all, your rent is only two days late. I just wanted to remind you in case you'd forgotten,' said the sweet old lady.

'My rent? Oh my rent . . .' he had replied. Then, testing the water, he had stood up again and said, 'I meant to apologise for my appearance.'

She looked him up and down and said, 'I think you look fine, Mr Dilly. Very smart. My Ivor never looked smart in his life. On our wedding day, the vicar threw him out of the church. He thought he was a tramp who had come in for the wine!'

Blind as a bat. And as mad as a badger. Since then Mrs K often popped in, always with some story about her dead husband, Ivor, and her children, who were grown up now and never visited. The old girl liked the company and Dirk was always careful not to let his scaly skin accidentally brush against her.

★ ★ ★

Dirk took his usual route south, leaping from roof to roof, ever grateful that dragons cast shadows upwards. Still, he had to be careful, particularly in South London, where the buildings were lower to the ground. The consequences of being seen were unthinkable. But he was quick and humans were slow. He had been doing this job long enough to know that he could avoid being seen as long as he stayed alert.

He arrived at Elliot Drive. It was the kind of quiet suburban area that human families liked to live in. Half of its inhabitants would be crammed into over-flowing trains on their way home from boring office jobs, wondering what was for dinner. The other half would be at home cooking dinner, thinking about how nice it would be to have a job to get them out of the house.

He ran across a row of terraced houses, jumping the chimneys like they were hurdles, then somer-saulted across the quiet road and landed on number forty-three. He curled himself around a chimney, pulled out his pad, flicked it open and checked his notes.

Female Cat - black - white paws - white face, black smudge
Answers to name 'Willow'

* * *

He watched a tabby stroll across a garden proudly. Another, this one ginger, darted from a cat flap, chasing an imaginary mouse. Dirk raised his head, seeing a black cat stretching on the warmth of a car bonnet, but its paws were black, too, and its face wasn't white.

And then he saw just about the last thing he had ever expected to see. At first he noticed the smoke coming from a chimney three streets away, just above where the black cat was rolling on the car. But looking more closely he saw that the smoke wasn't coming from the house. Curled around the chimney, was a red-backed, green-bellied Mountain Dragon lying quietly on the roof. It was like looking in a mirror. He couldn't believe it. Was it lost? Did it know the punishment for being seen by a human? What was it doing here?

Suddenly, the other dragon swooped down from the rooftop and then back up again. It jumped to another building and then another and so on, travelling much in the same way as Dirk did.

The black cat, that seconds ago had been lying so contentedly and happily in the sun, was gone. That's what the dragon was doing there. It was stealing cats.

The next question, of course, was why?

Chapter Three

Dirk took chase. The other Mountain Dragon obviously wasn't expecting to be followed, so Dirk was able to stay close behind, but every now and then it would pause on a rooftop, waiting for someone to pass, and he would have to stop dead in his tracks to avoid being seen.

Until that moment he knew of only one other dragon living in the area, but he dwelt far below the surface and would never be seen jumping around on rooftops in broad daylight.

On the whole, dragons were solitary creatures living in isolation high up in the mountains, deep within the oceans or far beneath the surface of the earth. There were no dragon towns or cities. Living in London, Dirk marvelled at so many humans wanting to cram themselves into such a small space. It was no wonder they were so unpleasant to each other most of the time.

But despite the greed, deceit and corruption that Dirk uncovered daily, he loved the city with its historic buildings, bright lights, constant noise and variety of smells – some great, like popcorn or fast food, some bad, like car-exhaust fumes or fish markets on hot days. He had been there so long that it was now as much a part of him as his own wings.

Dirk had followed the mystery dragon all the way to the River Thames and was now heading eastward, where the roofs were higher and wider, the trees fewer and the buildings greyer.

And then it vanished. One minute it was on top of an old warehouse in the middle of a particularly grim-looking industrial estate. The next, it had disappeared from sight.

Cautiously he approached the spot where the other dragon had stood. He landed lightly on the rooftop and scanned it for clues. On the flat roof was a dirty skylight that looked down into the warehouse below. He wiped the dirt away with one paw, being careful not to scratch the glass with his razor-sharp talons, and peered in.

In the warehouse below were five large wooden crates. Four of them had the words **DO NOT OPEN** printed in red on the top. The fifth crate, in the middle of the room read, **HANDLE WITH CARE**.

A bell rang and a door opened at the side of the building. A short, fat man entered, and walked to the middle crate.

'Blimey,' he said, straining to lift it. 'It's like tryin' to lift a flippin' lead-lined elephant. Lend us an 'and, will you?'

'A hand?' replied a second man, entering the building.

He was taller than the first, with the merest wisp of hair carefully combed across his otherwise bald head. 'May I remind you that you are supposed to be the muscles of this operation?'

'Can't you just take one corner?'

'No, I cannot. As I have explained to you some thirty-eight times now, I am unable to participate in any physical activity on account of a rare condition that I concocted in Africa. That is why I am the brains.'

'I think I wanna be the brains for a change. Maybe

we could job share,' panted the fat man.

'Sadly, my friend, that would require you being in possession of the aforementioned grey matter to which you have previously referred,' said the tall man.

'Eh?'

'You're too thick. Now come on!'

'Honestly, I'm gonna give meself an 'ernia if I keep on like this. Why can't we get a forklift truck?'

'What would I use a forklift truck for?'

'Movin' the boxes.'

'I see, so I could drive in, lift up the boxes using my forklift truck, move them hither and thither and I wouldn't even have to disturb you from your beauty sleep.'

'Exactly.'

'Then what would I need you for?'

'Oh . . . I didn't think of that.'

'Which is why I do the thinking.'

'I could make the tea.'

A bell rang, making Dirk jump. He looked around but couldn't see any sign of danger. The bell rang for ten seconds and then stopped. He put his ear back to the roof.

'Come on, let's go,' said the taller man. 'Leave that.'

The short, fat man put the crate down and said,

'Why do we have to leave every time that bell goes off?'

'While I'm the brains, leave the whys to me. OK?'

'Look, I ain't grumbling. I'm glad to have a break. It's just that every time that blinking bell . . .'

The rest of his words were cut off by the bell, which rang again. By the time it had finished the two men had left the building.

Dirk looked up and saw, just in time, another dragon approaching. This one was light grey and in place of ears had two gills. It was a Sea Dragon. But this was no time to get out his *I Spy Book of Dragons*. It was coming this way, bounding across the roofs towards him.

Quick as a flash he leapt in the air and somersaulted backwards over the edge of the building. Grabbing wildly, he caught hold of a gutter by the tip of his claws. With a loud CLANK the Sea Dragon landed on the roof. Dirk held his breath. Had he been seen? He could hear the other dragon pacing on the roof centimetres away from him. Was he trying to work out where he had gone?

The plastic gutter creaked unhappily. Clearly it wasn't designed to support the weight of a dragon, even one in as good shape as Dirk. He looked down.

Directly below him was a mass of barbed wire on top of the high fence that separated the yard beside the warehouse from the main road. The two men were walking across the yard towards an old caravan.

'I mean, every time that bell goes off, we have to evacuate. It's a bit odd, if you ask me,' the fat man was saying.

'No one would, or indeed should, ask you. And I am certain that no one did. Now, I believe you mentioned tea.'

Dirk could smell the other dragon's sulphurous breath. He heard the soft miaow of a cat.

The guttering had completely come away from the building now and, rather than holding on to it, Dirk was flapping his wings, hovering mid-air, holding it up, desperately trying to stop it from falling. But there was too much of it. It was going to fall, and when it did it would attract the attention of the two idiotic men and that would draw their eyes to him. There was only one thing for it. He had to get back on the roof. Better to confront a dragon than be seen by humans.

Here goes, he thought.

One . . .

Two . . .

Three.

In one swift movement he let go of the gutter, somersaulted up on to the roof and landed on his hind legs, claws drawn, ready to fight.

There was no one there. The dragon had gone. The drainpipe clattered noisily to the ground. He edged back to the glass and looked down into the warehouse. Nothing. Just the five crates. The dragon was nowhere in sight. He could hear the two men come out of the caravan.

'What's happenin'?' said one.

'This place is falling apart,' replied the other. 'Now where's my tea?'

Dirk was shaken. There was something very odd going on. And whatever it was, it was far bigger than one lost cat. That was for sure.

Chapter Four

Back in the safety of his office, Dirk sat behind his desk, picked up a remote control and switched on the old television that sat on a filing cabinet on the other side of the room. Dirk loved his TV. It was from watching late-night movies that he had first got the idea of becoming a detective. He flicked through the channels. There was nothing on. A woman on a shopping channel held up an apparently revolutionary new duster. 'Look around your room,' she squeaked annoyingly. 'Can you see all that dust?'

Dirk glanced at the piles of old newspapers and files from previous cases. 'I can't even see the floor,' he replied, switching it off.

Cats, he thought. *Why cats*? In spite of what humans have written throughout history, dragons are and always have been vegetarians. Humans saw the big teeth, the sharp claws and the ability to breathe fire and assumed they were carnivores like themselves. In fact, eating meat was agony to dragons. It made their blood boil, like being cooked from the inside. If a dragon ate enough, its blood would turn to gas and it would die. Dirk didn't like the sound of this at all, so tended a stick to cans of baked beans and self-toasted bread.

This investigation was going to be far more involved than he had previously thought. He picked up the phone and dialled his client's number. A deep male voice answered the phone.

'Malcolm Bigsby, MP. Hello,' it boomed.

'Hi, can I speak to Holly?'

'Who?' barked the man.

There was a click as another phone was picked up and a girl's voice said, 'Dad, it's for me.'

'Oh yes. That Holly. Right, sorry.'

Another click indicated the first phone had been put down.

'Is that Mr Dilly?' asked Holly.

'Yes, look your cat . . .'

'Willow. Have you found her? Is she all right?'

'Well, no . . .'

'Is she hurt?'

'No . . .'

'So she's all right?'

'Look, if you'll let me explain,' yelled Dirk down the receiver, fed up of being interrupted.

Holly fell silent and Dirk realised that he had made the phone call without the faintest idea of what he was going to say. He could hardly tell her what had really happened: *Look, kiddo, your cat has been stolen by a dragon and taken to a warehouse in East London.* No, that wouldn't do at all.

'I . . . It's just that . . .' he started, 'it's going to take longer than I thought to find your cat.'

'Why?'

'Because . . . Because it just is. Look, I'll call when I've got news, but don't expect that to be too soon.'

'What's happened to her?' demanded Holly.

'I don't know. I honestly don't know.'

Dirk slammed down the phone. He turned to face the window, swivelled the blinds so that he could see the evening sky and contemplated the case. The cats, the dragons. The dragons, the cats. What was the link? What was the connection? There had to be a connection. Cats and dragons. Dragons and cats. After several hours of this sort of thinking and eight glasses of orange squash drunk neat, Dirk drifted off into an uneasy sleep.

He was halfway through a dream involving an army of flying cats carpet-bombing London with exploding fur balls when he was woken by a terrible banging.

'Take cover!' He awoke with a start. 'Who? What? Where?' he exclaimed.

'Mr Dilly?' It was Mrs Klingerflim. 'Mr Dilly,' she called, banging noisily on the door.

'It's open,' replied Dirk, rubbing his eyes, and squinting in the early morning sunlight. He must have slept all night.

The door edged open and Mrs Klingerflim's owl-like face appeared around it. 'Sorry to disturb you, but your niece is here.'

'What?'

'Come along, dear,' she said, pushing the door open.

'No,' yelled Dirk. 'She can't come in.'

'What's that?' said the old lady.

Dirk leapt off the seat and dived under the desk,

squeezing his large body into the small space.

'Thank you, Mrs Klingerflim,' replied a girl's voice.

'What a polite girl,' said Mrs Klingerflim. 'What did you say your name was?'

'Holly,' said the girl.

Through a hole in the desk Dirk saw a pair of green trainers and green socks enter the room. 'Uncle Dirk? Where are you?' called the girl.

Dirk said nothing, frozen.

'Well,' said Mrs Klingerflim. 'I'll leave you two to catch up. Don't forget your rent is due next week, Mr Dilly.' The door closed.

Dirk thought fast. What were his options? There was no way to escape without being seen. People tend to notice when a four-metre-long (from tail to nose) red-backed, green-bellied, urban-based Mountain Dragon crawls out from under a desk and leaves the room. He would have to stay hidden and bluff his way out of this.

'What a dump,' said Holly. 'What are you doing under the desk?'

'I dropped my pen,' said Dirk.

'Has there been a fire?'

'Yes, just a little one. I dropped a cigarette.'

'You shouldn't smoke. It's very bad for you.'

'I know, I'm trying to give up,' he replied frostily.

'Dad's big-haired wife smokes sometimes,' said the girl. 'She doesn't think anyone knows but I've checked in her handbag and she's always got a packet. I always take them out and throw them away, but she never says anything because that would be like admitting it and it would involve talking to me. Dad doesn't notice that she smells of smoke, but then he doesn't really notice anything at all. They think I'm at school today.'

'Shouldn't you be at school?' snapped Dirk.

'This is far more important. I want to know what's happened to my cat, Willow.'

'How did you find me? My address isn't in the phone book.' Dirk felt pins and needles crawl through his tail from being so cramped in the small space.

'You'd be amazed how much information you can get from the Internet. Have you found your pen yet?'

'There seem to be quite a lot down here. I may be some time. You might as well go away and I'll call you later.'

'Are you sure you're not hiding?'

'Of course not. Why do you say that?'

'I've just never known anyone to spend so much

time under a desk. It's a bit odd.'

'What do you want?' Dirk asked.

'I want to know what's happened to my cat?'

'It's difficult to explain. Look, kiddo, you have to leave.'

'I'll leave when you come out from under that desk.'

'I can't.'

'Why?'

'I just can't.'

'Then I'm not leaving.'

'Look, you're trespassing. You lied about who you were and illicitly gained access to my office. Get out!' demanded Dirk.

'You call this tip an office?'

Dirk was seriously annoyed. It was one thing to come barging in, uninvited. It was another to impersonate a family member. But he wasn't going to stand for – or in this case, hide under a desk for – a complete stranger calling his office a tip. Sure, it needed a bit of a tidy up. And perhaps he hadn't taken out the rubbish for a couple of days, or possibly weeks. But this was his home.

Angrily Dirk said, 'I'll call your parents and tell them you're not at school.'

'Go on, then,' challenged Holly. 'The phone's on the desk.'

Dirk growled quietly to himself. 'If you don't go away I won't tell you what happened to your cat,' he said.

After a moment's silence Holly sighed and said, 'All right, I'll go. But I want to know what's going on. Call me.'

'It's a deal,' said Dirk and he watched the green shoes disappear out of sight and heard the door close. She had gone. Breathing a sigh of relief he edged his way backwards and climbed up from under the desk. He stretched himself out and cricked his back. 'Oh, that's better,' he muttered to himself, rubbing his numb tail.

'You're a dragon,' said a small, surprised voice.

Dirk looked down and saw a brown-haired, brown-eyed girl standing by the door, staring up at him.

'Rats,' he said, 'Big baskets of fat rats called Albert!'

Chapter Five

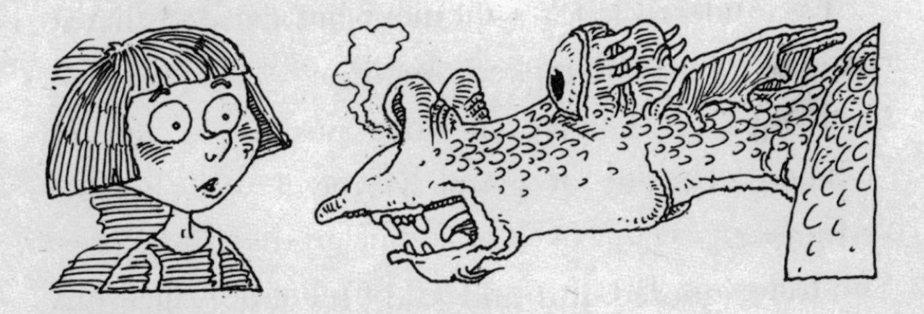

At least she's not screaming, thought Dirk. Instead of screaming, Holly was standing frozen to the spot, eyes as wide as golf balls, mouth as wide as a football, looking as though she had just seen the exact last thing she expected to see at that exact moment in time. Her brown hair hung in a neat bob. Dressed in a red T-shirt, orange jeans and green socks and trainers, she put Dirk in mind of a set of traffic lights.

'What are you staring at?' he demanded.

'I mean, I just thought it was a cool name, the Dragon Detective Agency. I thought maybe you'd be Welsh or something. You know, they have a dragon on their flag, but I noticed you didn't have a Welsh accent, but I thought maybe . . . I just thought it was a cool name. I never thought you actually were a dragon,' said Holly.

'No kidding. That's kind of the idea, kiddo. Why aren't you screaming?'

'I considered it for a moment but decided that it wouldn't help,' she replied simply.

'I think if I were in your position a scream wouldn't be out of place. Maybe a yelp. Even a whimper.'

Holly ignored this and said, 'It's just brilliant. A dragon. Can you fly?'

'Of course I can fly. What do you think these are for?' he snarled, flapping his wings, 'Air conditioning?'

'And breathe fire?'

Dirk picked up the top page of a newspaper from his desk and, showing off, rolled it up, pursed his lips and exhaled. A tiny line of fire darted out and set it alight.

'Wow!' exclaimed Holly. 'Cool.'

In an instance the paper burnt down to his paw. 'Ow!' yelled Dirk, placing his finger in his mouth. The lit piece of paper floated down to the desk, where it landed on the rest of the newspaper, setting the whole thing alight.

'Rats,' he said, trying to put out the fire with his paw. 'Ow!' he said, whipping it away again. The fire meanwhile was growing and blackening the desk. 'I'll blow it out,' said Dirk and he drew a deep breath and blew.

'No!' shouted Holly, but it was too late. Another line of fire came from his mouth, just making matters worse.

Dirk growled in frustration. 'Stand back,' he said. He shut his eyes and threw himself over the fire. With a crash the desk collapsed beneath his weight. The fire, however, was finally out.

'Super rats from Mars,' said Dirk, looking up to see Holly clutching her sides, bent over, laughing.

'You're funny,' she said.

'Oh, I'm glad I amuse you, kiddo,' said Dirk coldly. 'That's really what I was aiming for. Just think of me as part uncle, part dragon, part clown. Now, if you don't mind, I've got work to do.'

'To find Willow?'

'Your cat isn't my only case,' lied Dirk.

'But what about Willow?'

'Listen. In the grand scheme of things one missing cat doesn't add up to a hill of beans. It's not exactly the crown jewels, is it?'

'She's more important to me.'

'My heart is bleeding.'

'But you must know something otherwise you wouldn't have phoned to say it was going to take longer than you thought.'

'You don't let up, do you?'

'Anyway, what's a dragon doing working as a detective?'

'I'm so sorry you don't approve of my career choice. I suppose you think I should have got a nice job in a bank.'

'Don't be silly.'

'Don't call me silly.' If there was one thing Dirk hated more than being laughed at, it was being called silly. This girl was really annoying him. 'You have to go now. You shouldn't have seen me, but I'll let you get away with it because you're only a kid. Who's going to believe you?'

'No way. I'm helping you find Willow.'

'What do you know about being a detective?'

'I found you, didn't I?'

This was true. Dirk didn't exactly make it easy for clients to find where he was located. 'You're only eleven. You're too young.'

'Just because I'm young, I'm still smart.'

'And modest.'

'Why? How old are you?' she replied.

'One thousand, two hundred and sixty-seven next July.'

'Wow, that's really old.'

'Watch it. That's quite young for a dragon and I think I'm in pretty good shape for my age, actually. I like to keep myself trim,' said Dirk, holding his stomach in.

'I could be your sidekick like Dr Watson and Sherlock Holmes.'

'I live alone and I work alone.' Dirk sat behind his broken desk. 'That's the way it's always been and that's the way I like it.'

'Don't you have any friends?' said Holly, pulling up a chair and sitting down opposite him.

'Dragons aren't that big on friends.'

'What about your family?'

'Let's not get too personal now.'

'Well, I think it sounds very lonely.'

'What about you?' said Dirk, turning on Holly. 'Your dad didn't seem to have even heard of you.'

'He's very busy,' she replied defensively. 'He's a junior minister now.'

'And you've got lots of friends, have you?'

'I've got Willow,' she replied. 'She's my best friend.'

Dirk snorted. 'She's a cat,' he said dismissively.

'She's still my friend. I like animals. They're more reliable than people.'

'Don't children normally have friends at school?'

'I change schools a lot, so I never make any new friends and if I do I just leave again and then they're lost, so I don't bother any more.'

'That sounds very lonely,' Dirk said pointedly, but instantly regretted it as Holly's brown eyes welled up with tears. If there was one thing he really couldn't deal with it was a blubbing human. 'Come on,' he said awkwardly. 'It's all right. Don't cry.'

'Will you let me help you find Willow?' Holly's voice wavered.

'I can't . . .'

Holly's head fell into her hands, her shoulders began to shake and the loud piercing wail started. It was a horrible sound.

'Anything the matter?' called Mrs Klingerflim's voice from the hallway.

'No nothing, Mrs K,' replied Dirk. 'Look, shut up. All right. Stop. You can come along,' he said without thinking.

'On . . . the . . . investigation?' Holly managed to utter in between sobs.

'All right, but only today.'

'What . . . are . . . you doing today?' she said tearfully.

'Today is the stakeout.'

The sobbing noise stopped instantly and Holly said, 'Stake-out. Cool!' Wow, where are we going?'

'But that's it,' said Dirk, a tad suspicious of Holly's instant recovery. 'Then you leave the detective work to the dragon, OK?'

'Absolutely,' said Holly and, as if sensing his suspicion, she looked away and wiped a tear from her eye. 'You won't regret this, Mr Dilly,' she said.

'I've got a feeling I might,' replied Dirk.

Chapter Six

Dirk was regretting his decision, but he had said it now and if there was one thing that all those years of being a detective had shown him, it was that if your word was no good, then nor were you. However, he was beginning to wish that, just this once, he had made an exception to the rule. The girl had an endless line of annoying questions. 'What do you eat? Where were you born? How long have you lived in London? Has anyone ever seen you before?'

He batted each one off with a non-committal grunt. The less she knew the better. He hadn't even told her about the dragons he had seen stealing the cats. He figured he could take her out today as he had promised and then she would leave him alone.

'How do you avoid being seen? Can you turn invisible?' asked Holly, finding it difficult to mask her excitement.

'Invisible, no,' replied Dirk. 'We avoid being seen by taking the high road. Now shut up and climb on my back.'

Holly clambered on. His back was hard like armour, but as she climbed on she accidentally kicked him in his soft, green underbelly.

'Ow,' he grumbled. 'Watch what you're doing. I'm not a bouncy castle. Hold on tight.'

Holly squeezed her arms tightly around the dragon's neck.

'Noh thah tight,' Dirk said in a strangulated whisper.

'Sorry,' said Holly, loosening her grip.

Dirk checked that the coast was clear then pulled the blind up and threw open the window.

'Try not to make any noise,' he said, leaping out, with Holly clinging on to his back. They landed on the roof across the road from his office and Holly surveyed the rooftops of London.

'Wow,' she exclaimed loudly in Dirk's ear, 'this is brilliant.'

'Be quiet! Do you know what would happen if we were seen?'

'Sorry,' she said more quietly.

Dirk leapt to the next roof.

'Would they put you in a zoo?'

'A zoo? Put me in a zoo? I'd like to see them try. Hold on, this is a big one.'

He soared high into the sky and landed on an office block, scampered along the flat roof and jumped to the next building.

'What would happen if you were seen, then?' asked Holly.

'Rats. Window cleaners,' said Dirk, turning and changing direction. 'We'd better take the long route.' He leapt to another nearby rooftop and then another. With each jump he stretched out his wings, enabling him to glide to the next building without his footsteps landing so heavily as to be heard below.

'What would happen if you were seen?' Holly persisted.

'Stay very still,' he said, coming to a very sudden halt on a rooftop. Before she could ask why, Holly heard a clattering mechanical sound getting louder and louder. A police helicopter flew towards them. She looked down at the dragon and to her surprise saw that Dirk's red back was the same colour and pattern as the rooftop upon which he was sitting. He was still there, breathing below her, his wings by his side, his eyes, looking furtively ahead, and yet he was, well, roof-coloured. The helicopter flew overhead, unaware of the dragon below.

'I thought you said you couldn't turn invisible,' she said.

'That's not invisible,' replied Dirk. 'That's just blending.'

'How do you do it?' she asked.

'It's not that difficult,' said Dirk, standing up on all fours, returning to his natural colour. 'You just have to stay very still and think like a roof.'

'But what would have happened if you were seen?'

'If humans knew that dragons existed?'

'Yes.'

They continued on their journey. 'There would be a war,' he said casually, 'dragons against humans.'

'But dragons are much stronger than humans, surely you'd win.'

'Individually we're stronger, yes. But humans have weapons that can wipe out entire cities. I may have a tough back, but drop a nuclear bomb on me and see what good it does.'

Dirk landed heavily on a supermarket roof and Holly let out a small yelp and grabbed his ears tightly.

'Ow!' said Dirk irritably. 'Ow and sh!'

'What about Mrs Klingerflim? She knows you're a dragon.'

'Mrs Klingerflim can't see further than the end of her own spectacles. Why else would she think you could be my niece?'

They were winging their way eastward. Holly sat up, relaxing a little. 'How many dragons are there in London, for example?' she asked.

'Look, kiddo, it's bad enough that you've seen me. I'm not answering any more questions. I said you can come with me today, then you can let me get back to doing my job.'

'Well, I didn't think that dragons existed at all until this morning.'

'You never wondered about the Loch Ness monster?'

Holly gasped. 'Why? Does it really exist? Is it a dragon?'

'No,' said Dirk, laughing. 'There's nothing in Loch Ness except fish and water.'

'Oh,' said Holly, disappointed. 'What about Saint George?'

'You call him Saint George. We just call him George the cold-blooded murderer. He killed a defenceless pregnant mother. Very heroic. Nice guy to choose for your patron saint,' snapped Dirk angrily.

'I didn't choose him. Don't have a go at me,' she replied.

'Hey, look, if you've had enough . . .' Dirk stopped on a sloping roof. He lowered his body by the chimney top and said, 'You can get off here and I can go about my business on my own. You run and tell your mummy and daddy that you met a dragon and he told you that the Loch Ness monster is just a rubbish story made up by scared humans. Go on, get off.'

'There's no need to be like that. I only pointed out you aren't very friendly, but it's to be expected, you don't have much company. Nor do I. Lots of people don't think I'm very nice either.'

'Don't you care?'

'Not really,' replied Holly. 'I know what I'm really like and if other people can't be bothered to find out then I can't be bothered to care what they think.'

Dirk craned his neck round to look at the girl. She looked stubbornly back at him.

'You're not like most humans,' he said. 'All my

clients ever care about is what other people think. They don't want it getting out that their wives are having affairs or that their business has gone under or that their daughters have run away from home. They want it kept quiet, brushed under the carpet.'

'Well, I just want to know what's happened to Willow. She's only a cat and can't really look after herself.'

'OK, then, let's find out.' Dirk stood up and they continued their journey in silence.

They came to rest on a flat factory rooftop across the road from the warehouse where he had seen the mysterious dragon take the cat. Lying in the yard outside the warehouse was the drainpiping that Dirk had ripped from the wall.

'Are we there?' asked Holly.

'Yes, get off,' he replied.

She clambered off his back and stretched her arms out. 'You're not very comfortable.'

'I'm not very friendly, I'm not very comfortable. It's a wonder you're here at all.'

'I told you, I . . .'

'Want to find your cat. Yes, yes, yes. Well, this is how we find her. We wait here and watch.'

'OK,' said Holly and she sat down. 'What are we watching?'

'That building.'

For an hour, they stared at the warehouse, but nothing happened. No dragons landed on the roof. Nobody went in or out of the building. Dirk was expecting Holly to moan about being bored. In fact, he was hoping she would. That way he could be shot of her. People always thought detective work was exciting but in reality most of it was like this. Sitting still, watching nothing happen slowly. He glanced at her, but she showed no signs of getting tired. Her eyes stared at the building as unblinkingly as they had an hour ago.

She caught him looking at her and said, 'What?'

'Nothing,' said Dirk

Suddenly a loud BANG rang out.

'Get down,' shouted Dirk, diving on top of Holly, pulling her to the floor.

'Get off,' she said.

'Don't be stupid. Somebody's shooting.'

'No, they're not,' she said, struggling beneath his heavy belly.

'Listen, kiddo. I've been in this business long enough to recognise a gun shot.'

'Then, how do you explain that?' she said, wrestling herself free and pointing down to the street. Dirk raised his head slowly and cautiously and saw a dirty once-white van, emitting more smoke than an angry Firedrake on a cold day. It rattled unhealthily down the road then with another loud BANG came to a stop outside the barbed-wire surround.

'That was close,' Holly laughed.

'Very amusing,' said Dirk, looking very unamused.

Two men stepped out of either side of the van.

'I think we need a new van, boss,' said the short, fat man.

'This mode of transportation meets all of the vehicular requirements of our current engagement, vis-à-vis the transportation of undisclosed items from hither and inevitably to thither,' said the taller man pompously.

'Come again?' The fat man looked perplexed.

'It still works.'

'Oh yeah, right,' the other man said.

Holly noticed that Dirk's ears had pricked up and he was staring intently at the two men.

'Who are they?' she asked.

'Suspects,' he replied through gritted teeth.

Chapter Seven

The taller man took a key from his pocket and opened the large padlock that kept the gate shut. The shorter, fatter man drove the van into the yard, climbed out and entered the warehouse. He emerged carrying a large and, judging by the redness of his face, very heavy wooden crate, with the words **HANDLE WITH CARE** printed on the outside.

'Flippin' 'eck, this is 'eavy, Arthur. What do you suppose they're all for, anyway?' asked the short, fat man.

'Ours is not to reason why, Reg. Ours is but to do and die,' replied the man called Arthur before adding smugly, 'Shakespeare.'

Reg dropped the crate into the back of the van, causing the forlorn vehicle to dip unhappily with its new burden.

'I don't get poetry,' he said, leaning against the van. 'I can't see why people can't just say what they mean. I mean, a poet will go on about his lady's eyes, saying they're like windows or stars or chocolate truffles or something, but really they're just eyes and if they're like anything it's other eyes because they're all eyes. You can't change what something is, can you?'

'What a fascinating thesis. Thank you, Reg. Tell me, are you familiar with the word ignoramus?'

'Course,' said Reg. 'It's a big lizard. My uncle Phil had one. But it bit him on the bum, so he shot it. Made a right mess. Aunt Dot weren't too pleased with him on account of it being a new carpet.'

'That's an iguana, Reg.'

'Oh right. What's that you said, then?'

'You, my friend, are an ignoramus. Now shut the doors and let's go. You know how particular Mr G is about the schedule.'

'You ask me, there's something funny about Mr G.'

'I didn't ask you to do anything other than lift and drive. Come on.'

'How come we never seen him, then?' Reg said,

slamming the back doors of the van and walking round to the front. The two men climbed in.

They pulled the doors shut and their voices cut out.

The van moaned and spluttered reluctantly but eventually the engine turned over. Dirty smoke billowed from the exhaust pipe and the van, the two men and the crate drove away.

'Come on,' said Dirk, 'get on.'

'Are we going to follow it?' asked Holly eagerly.

'Yes. Quickly.'

She scrambled on to his back and clasped her hands behind his ears. Dirk surveyed the rooftops and, satisfied he had a route, leapt to the next building, and then the next in pursuit of the van.

They followed the van through the London streets, further east along the River Thames. The smoke and loud banging noises that it produced made it easy to follow from some distance. But as they headed out of London, the buildings were lower and there were fewer of them. The landscape changed from the built-up narrow streets of London to a more sprawling, barren industrial area. A thin sheet of white cloud covered the sky. It was getting cold and Holly wished she had something warmer than her cardigan. She wrapped herself close to Dirk, hoping to steal some of his body heat, but found that his hard, scaly back was not actually very warm at all. And still the van rattled along the road.

Dirk was making bigger leaps than he had in the city, jumping high into the air and then gliding down towards the next building.

With a screech of the brakes, the van turned left off the main road and headed down a tree-lined dirt track to the riverside. Dirk's descent took him on to a rooftop of an old disused church by the road. He came to a sudden halt.

'Why have we stopped?' asked Holly.

'There aren't any buildings down there,' said Dirk, indicating where the van had gone.

'Can't you use the trees?'

'No, I can't. I'm a Mountain Dragon, not a Tree Dragon. Trees tend to bend or break when I land on them and there's not enough cover to fly over.'

'But we can't see what they're doing,' complained Holly.

The van and the two men were obscured behind the small wooded area, overgrown through neglect, and they were well out of earshot.

'We'll just have to wait until they move on again,' replied Dirk. 'I can't risk being seen. I've told you what would happen.'

'That's rubbish,' said Holly.

Dirk snarled, 'It's called being a detective, waiting for the right moment, staying out of sight. Sometimes you just have to be patient.'

'But we might miss something important!' Holly exclaimed urgently.

'Have you got a better idea?' snapped Dirk.

'I'll go,' said Holly.

'What?'

'I'm small. I'll sneak up and see what they're up to.'

Dirk considered this. He didn't really want this human any more involved than she already was, but it was true, she was small. And he had to admit that it would be useful to know what those two crooks were up to.

'All right,' he said. 'But stay out of sight.'

'I will.'

'And don't let them hear you.'

'I won't.'

'And be careful crossing the road.'

'Hurry up,' snapped Holly impatiently. 'They're opening the van.'

'OK.' Dirk surveyed the road. There was nothing coming. There was no one else around. He swooped down to the ground. Holly jumped off his back and he returned to the safety of the roof.

He watched as Holly looked both ways then crossed the road. She ran up the path towards the van. He strained to see what the two men were doing, but it was no use. Dragon eyesight was good, but not good enough to see through the overgrown trees that swayed lightly in the cold evening breeze. Halfway down the track Holly turned, gave him the thumbs-up and then disappeared off the track into the trees.

'What am I doing letting a human kid help me?' Dirk asked himself. 'I must be going soft in the head.'

Chapter Eight

Making her way through the undergrowth, Holly approached the van. Her heart beat fast. She felt scared, exhilarated. She could see the men more clearly now, but what with the crunching of the leaves and the snapping twigs beneath her feet it was extremely difficult to move quietly. Luckily the fat man called Reg was moaning loudly enough to cover her as she scuttled forwards.

'This'll be the fourth crate this week, and they ain't getting any lighter. I'll do myself an injury if I'm not careful.'

Holly dived behind a nearby bush and found a place where she could peel back a branch and watch as well as listen to the two men. She could see the van parked alongside the river, its back doors open. The ground sloped down to where the high-tide river lapped at the muddy bank. A raft bobbed on the river, connected to the shore by a long rope, the other end of which was tied to a wooden post.

'Quit your moaning and haul it in,' said the man called Arthur, pointing at the raft.

The fat man grabbed the rope and pulled it towards the shore.

'I mean, it's not a normal job, is it? I been doin' this sort of caper for I don't know how long and I ain't never had a job like this before.' He wound the rope around the post as the raft got nearer.

'My advice to you would be to stop worrying about the whys and focus on the remunerative benefits of the assignment,' said Arthur.

'The what?'

'The money, Reg. The money.'

'Oh, well. The money's good, I'll give you that.'

'Good? For the sort of money we're getting for this job Mr G could ask me to paint myself with black-and-white stripes, dowse myself in tomato ketchup and jump into a cage full of peckish lions. And I would happily oblige, no questions asked.'

'Only you'd probably get me to do it,' moaned Reg.

'That is the unique and peculiar nature of our partnership, yes, but you have to remember, without me Mr G wouldn't entrust us with such an important task.'

The raft was by the riverbank now.

'He says it's important. You say it's important. But what's it important for? I'd rather be doing a good honest bank job or breaking and entering or just breaking. Because at least with those things you understand what you're doing it for.'

'If understanding is so essential to you I am astonished you do anything at all,' replied Arthur, with a snide smirk.

Reg secured the rope round the wooden post, walked over to the van and jumped in the back. The vehicle shuddered under the strain of the man's bulk.

'Mr G is a very brilliant man,' said Arthur. 'Whatever his reasons are I guarantee they are very brilliant.'

Reg stumbled out of the van, clutching the large crate, his short chubby arms covering the words **HANDLE WITH CARE**. He stepped on to the muddy ground and instantly lost his footing, staggering forward and dropping the crate, which landed in front of him and slid down towards the water's edge, dragging the fat man with it. There was a big splash and for a moment Holly thought Reg had fallen in the water. In fact, he had somehow landed with the crate and the top half of his body on the raft, but with his feet still on the edge of the riverbank. His large belly wobbled dangerously over the water between land and raft.

'Oh, bother,' he said. 'Can you get the rope and pull me back in, please?'

'Sorry, Reg. No can do. You see, I have a rare but pathological fear of rope. More of a dread than a fear, really. A mortal dread is what I have of rope and all rope matter.'

'I didn't know that,' said Reg, trying not to let the up and down movement of the crate drag him into the river.

'Oh yes. I caught it in India, while watching an old Indian rope trick known as "Biriani Poppadum Masala", which translates as "Rope trick that is both Indian and old". I've never been able to so much as touch a rope since. It ruined my dream of becoming a sailor. I'm all right with string funnily enough.'

While Arthur was saying this, Reg had managed to

bend his legs, arch his back, lean backwards, and successfully free himself of his dilemma, remaining completely dry. Looking pleased with himself, he brushed himself down, unwound the rope and carefully kicked the raft so that the crate bobbed out on to the river.

'Well done, Reg,' said Arthur, slapping him on the back with such force that the fat man flew head first into the river with a loud SPLASH.

Holly suppressed a giggle, but Arthur didn't find it at all funny. 'Stop messing about,' he said. 'It's time to go.'

'Sorry, Arthur,' said Reg, treading water, then climbing up the muddy bank. 'I must have slipped.' He was soaking wet, with streaks of mud down his face and clothes.

Caught by the river's current, the raft and large crate bobbed out into the middle of the river, pulling the rope taut.

The two men returned to the van.

'Can we go to my place so I can change my clothes?' asked Reg.

'What's wrong with those ones?' demanded Arthur.

'They're all wet.'

'Well, you should have thought about that before you decided to go for a swim, shouldn't you?'

They climbed into the van, closed the doors and, after some protest from the engine, drove away.

Holly jumped out from her hiding place and ran to the river's edge. She looked at the raft bobbing on the river. She listened. To her horror, she could hear the unmistakable sound of cats miaowing. She gasped.

The crate was full of cats.

She grabbed the rope and tugged at it, but it wouldn't budge. Far out on the water she could hear desperate feline pleas coming from the crate. *Those poor cats*, she thought, *they must be terrified. What was going to happen to them?* She needed to rescue them, but how? She needed Dirk.

Chapter Nine

Dirk was getting worried about Holly. Not that he cared what happened to the girl. Oh no. He was too tough and too old to get sentimental. And even if he did care a little, it was only because of the possible repercussions for him. It was one thing a cat going missing but a human girl was an entirely different matter. Besides, she had called him from home. The police only had to do a few checks and his number would come up, then they would start asking difficult questions, wanting to know his involvement. The police wouldn't leave it at a phone call either. They would want to actually come round and check out his office. Yes, it would only make life complicated if anything happened to her. That was the only reason he found himself hoping that Holly was OK.

His thoughts were disturbed by the sound of the reluctant once-white van chug-chug-chugging its way down the path, turning right on to the road and disappearing noisily into the distance.

A few seconds passed while Dirk stared intently ahead and then Holly appeared, her arms outstretched, running towards him, shouting at the top of her voice, 'Dirk! Help. Come now. You've got to help them.'

Amateur, thought Dirk. If there was one thing he knew about being a detective it was that no matter how bad things got, you always kept your nerve. You didn't go screaming blue murder at the first sign of problem.

'Dirk Dilly. You've got to save them!' she cried.

Cursing the girl, Dirk quickly checked that the coast was clear, spread his wings, jumped and glided across the road, down the tree-lined path, landing in front of her. He raised himself up on to his hind legs and said, 'Shut up, will you. Do you want everyone to know we're here?'

But Holly just grabbed Dirk's paw and dragged him towards the river. He looked across the water.

The area was fairly rundown this far from the city. On the north bank was an old rusty boat that looked like it hadn't been used in twenty years. Behind it was a shabby collection of ugly grey apartment blocks overlooking some overgrown allotments.

'What?' asked Dirk.

'It's full of cats,' said Holly, pointing to the crate floating in the middle of the river. 'Listen.'

Dirk listened and, sure enough, he could hear the desperate miaows drifting across the water.

'You've got to rescue them,' said Holly.

'Hey, kiddo. It's one thing me letting you tag along for a bit. But nobody orders the dragon around.'

'All right,' said Holly. 'Please can you rescue them?'

'That's better. Now let me see.' Dirk grabbed the rope and pulled. It didn't budge. He tried again, straining as he did. Nothing. 'It must have caught on something.'

'Can't you fly out and get it?' said Holly'.

'I think we're taking enough risks as it is without flying into open water in daylight.'

'Can't you swim out, then?'

'I think you may have confused me with a Sea Dragon. Easy mistake. Sea dragons have grey backs, shorter wings and they tend to be a little slimmer, although I like to think I keep myself in pretty good shape. But no, I'm more of your red-backed, green-bellied, urban-based Mountain Dragon. Not a big swimmer.'

'But what's going to happen to them? Willow might be in there and you promised you'd get her back.'

'Oh, all right.' Dirk gave in. 'I'll swim out and get the stupid moggies.'

'Thank you, Dirk.'

Dirk dropped on to all fours and cautiously approached the water's edge. It looked cold. It looked dirty. In fact, it looked about as inviting as a barrel of blue-skinned salamander sick, which, if you've never experienced such a thing, is not very inviting at all.

'Hurry up,' urged Holly before hastily adding, 'please.'

Dirk dipped his paw into the water. 'It's cold,' he said.

'Oh, come on,' said Holly, and she pushed against his large rear, catching him off guard and knocking him into the water with an enormous splash.

'Oh th . . . th . . . thanks,' shivered Dirk. 'I was just hoping someone would push me into a freezing-cold, filthy river.'

'No problem,' replied Holly, trying not to find it too amusing.

Dirk paddled through the cold and murky water towards the crate, thinking that he had been foolish to let the human tag along. She was already too involved. When he got back to shore he would take her home. No more Mr Nice Dragon. Dirk worked alone.

He reached the crate and circled it but was unable to see what it was caught on. The whole thing was very strange, dragons stealing cats, putting them in crates to be picked up by a pair of human crooks, who pushed them out on to the river. He had never heard of anything like it.

He closed his nostrils, ears and mouth and ducked his head under. Despite what he had said to Holly, Dirk, like all dragons, was capable of surviving for long periods of time underwater. Sea Dragons, like the one he had seen on the warehouse, often went centuries without surfacing, their backs softening with time to aid swimming.

The water was muddied and dark and the shadow cast by the raft made it even darker beneath it. Dirk couldn't see a thing. He groped around until he found something solid. It was long and smooth and appeared to be wrapped round the base of the raft. He tugged at it, but it wouldn't budge. He tried moving his hands down, but it seemed to go on for ever. If only he could see what he was doing. After several more unsuccessful attempts to free the raft, he lost patience. He opened his jaws and bit down. But instead of it snapping, as he had expected, he felt his teeth sink into it. It was soft like flesh, and something dark and rancid leaked from it, blackening the water. Instinctively Dirk let go. He reached to grab it again, but it had gone. Whatever it was it had let go.

Quickly he resurfaced, and paddled as fast as he could towards the shore, pushing the raft in front of him.

But he was feeling tired. His legs grew weak. Energy was draining away from him with each passing second. The raft grew heavier and heavier. He felt like he was swimming in treacle. Every stroke felt like his last.

I must be near now, he thought. He could hear Holly shouting, but he couldn't respond and his vision had gone as though night had fallen. Too tired. Even breathing was too much effort. Holly's face loomed in front of him.

'What's wrong?' he heard her say.

But the exhaustion had overrun every muscle in his body. He pulled himself on to the riverbank and tried to stand, but stumbled and then the darkness took him and he collapsed.

Chapter Ten

'Dirk,' screamed Holly. She shook the dragon's limp body, but he didn't respond. She lowered her head to listen to his heartbeat, but quickly realised that she had absolutely no idea where a dragon's heart might be kept. Providing they even had hearts. 'What's happened to you, Dirk? Can you hear me?'

He said nothing.

A miaow from the box reminded her about the cats. The crate bobbed by the side of the bank, but it was too heavy for her to lift. Instead she climbed on to the raft, edged her way carefully on to the other side and with all the energy she could muster, pushed.

The crate toppled over, causing an almighty screeching from within. Holly scrambled back on to the bank, rounded the crate and yanked open the top. Cats clambered out. More cats than she had ever seen in one place. Gingers, tabbies, black, white, grey, all scrambling over each other, desperate to get out of the crate on to dry land. Holly had never heard cats make such a noise. The poor things. They must have been terrified. And then at last she saw what she was looking for: a black cat with white paws and a white face with a black smudge on her nose. It was Willow. Holly reached down to grab her and received a scratch from another cat. Ignoring the pain, she picked Willow up.

'Willow,' she whispered, looking into the cat's eyes. 'You're alive.'

Willow replied with a sweet miaow.

Holly wrapped her arms round her cat and hugged her tightly. Willow purred. 'I'm so glad you're OK,' she said. Willow was more than a pet. She was more than a friend. She was Holly's family. Not like Dad, who gave her pocket money, or Dad's big-haired wife, who told her to turn her music down and go to bed. When Holly had had a bad day at school or if she was feeling lonely or sad, Willow was always there, comforting, loving and pleased to see her. Holly felt tears of relief fill her eyes. She blinked several times and swallowed hard to stop them from falling.

She remained like that, cuddling Willow, grateful that she was alive, until a low moan reminded her that they weren't alone. She looked up. The other cats had disappeared into the undergrowth or gone off in search of bowls of milk or kindly old people who would take pity on them.

The moan had come from Dirk.

'Dirk?' she said, seeing that one of his eyes was half open.

He let out another groan.

'Wink if you can hear me,' she said.

Slowly but surely the large eyelid closed.

Then opened again.

Holly knew she had to get him back to his office, out of danger. This, however, was not as easily done as it was thought. She had the unique problem of having to get herself, her cat and this rather large dragon back to central London without drawing any unwanted attention. This called for some serious thinking.

'I could call a cab,' Holly said to herself, finding it easier to think aloud, 'But they would definitely notice that one of the customers was a dragon.' She paced up and down, Willow held in her arms. 'Same goes for an ambulance or police.' A plastic bag floated past in the river. 'I could push him on to the raft and we could drift down the river.' But watching the bag, she quickly realised that the current ran east towards the sea, not west towards the city. 'Besides,' she said to herself. 'I would probably capsize it trying to get him on and drown him.'

She held Willow up and asked her, 'How can I get Dirk back to his office without him being seen?'

The cat replied with a helpful miaow, which she completely ignored.

Then she said, 'Without being seen. That's it. Of course.'

She put Willow down carefully and told her to, 'Stay there.' Then she grabbed as much foliage as she could gather and threw it over Dirk's body, which took some time, with him having so much body to cover. Eventually he was covered enough that if someone was to come strolling down the path they wouldn't instantly recognise what he was. However, it wasn't a great disguise and she knew she had to act fast, so she scooped up Willow again and ran up the path.

At the road, she turned right and kept running until eventually she came across a phone box. After making a phone call she returned to the entrance of the path by the road.

There she waited, ducking back behind a hedge to avoid being seen by passing cars, not wanting to attract any unwanted attention. After about half an hour she climbed out and stared down the road. Eventually she saw what she was looking for.

Coming down the road towards her, lurching dangerously from side to side and driving at around five miles an hour, was a pale blue, round-topped car. Behind it five cars, two vans and a supermarket lorry were all furiously beeping their horns.

Holly jumped up and down, waved her arms and shouted, 'Hey, I'm over here.'

The car turned on to the track, allowing its train of followers finally to pick up a decent speed. As they passed, each one yelled an obscenity at the driver of the blue car, but she remained unfazed, instead, rolling down her window and saying, 'Is that you, Holly? Where's your uncle?'

'Oh, Mrs Klingerflim, thank you so much for coming,' replied Holly.

'Don't you worry yourself, dear. I do like a nice

drive every once in a while. Everyone in London, though, is very impatient, don't you find?'

The last of the cars passed and the driver shouted something so obscene that Holly wasn't even sure what it meant.

'He's down this path,' said Holly, getting into the car. She lowered her voice to a whisper and added, 'He's in an awful state though. I think he's been drinking.'

'Oh dear,' replied the old lady, lifting off the hand-brake and driving the car down the path, 'Mr Klingerflim liked a drink, you know. He used to get very silly, though, did Ivor. I remember, he once got so drunk that he thought he was a sheep. A sheep, yes. He kept bleating and following me around and as I recall he refused to eat his lamb stew, saying that it would be cannibalism. Silly man.'

'Watch out!' shouted Holly as the car veered towards a tree, which Mrs Klingerflim narrowly avoided by swerving at the last minute.

'Don't you worry. I'm an excellent driver,' she said unconvincingly.

They stopped by the side of the mound of leaves and branches under which Dirk lay.

'Where's that uncle of yours? I don't know, getting

himself all drunk and disorderly at his age,' said Mrs Klingerflim.

'It's all right, I'll get him. You stay here,' said Holly, getting out of the car, leaving Willow in the passenger seat. She opened the back door, walked over to where Dirk lay and knocked the foliage off his body.

This was the tricky bit.

She knelt down beside him. 'Now, Dirk,' she said in his ear.

Another gentle groan indicated that he was still conscious.

'We need to get you back, and Mrs Klingerflim is here but I can't lift you into the back seat. I need you to get in. OK?'

Nothing.

'OK?'

Another groan.

'Is everything all right?' called Mrs Klingerflim.

'Oh yes,' replied Holly. 'I'm just helping him in.'

'This is a lovely little dog, you've got,' said the old lady, stroking Willow in such a way that caused the cat to scowl and purr angrily.

Holly lifted Dirk's large heavy head and said, 'Come on, let's get you home.'

For a second, Holly thought the plan wasn't going

to work. Dirk's body was heavy and limp. Then she felt the weight of his head ease and, slowly but surely, he stood on all fours. Together they crawled forward. They reached the car and Dirk dragged himself on to the back seat, like it was the last thing he would ever do.

'Oh, what a state,' pronounced Mrs Klingerflim. 'Drunk as a skunk. Just like poor Ivor used to get.'

Dirk managed to squeeze his large body into the back. Holly grabbed his tail and crammed it into the car after him.

'Did you bring a blanket, as I asked?' she said.

'In the boot, dear,' replied Mrs Klingerflim. Holly retrieved an old blanket from the boot and threw it over Dirk's body. She slammed the back door shut and climbed in the front, lifting a very relieved-looking Willow away from Mrs Klingerflim's hand.

'Home, dear?' she asked benignly.

'Yes, Mrs Klingerflim. Thank you, Mrs Klingerflim.'

'Such good manners,' said the old lady, starting up the engine and driving the car back up the path, narrowly avoiding hitting every possible tree on the way and then turning right on to the wrong side of the road. Holly screamed and Mrs Klingerflim casually swerved, just missing an oncoming truck. Peeking through her fingers, Holly wondered whether this had been such a good plan after all.

Chapter Eleven

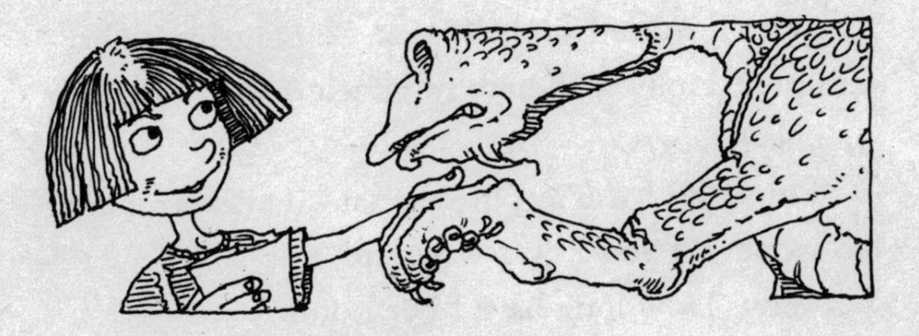

Dirk awoke from a terrible dream. He couldn't remember the details but he was left with a feeling of cold dread. He forced his heavy eyelids open and found himself staring up at his own ceiling.

He looked around. He was slumped in the corner of his office on the mattress where he normally slept. How had he got there? Waking up with no memory of the previous night was not entirely unheard of but it usually coincided with having drunk three bottles of pure, undiluted orange squash. He didn't recall having hit the concentrate last night, though.

Last night, he thought, *what happened last night?*

His office door swung open and Holly strode in,

her arms piled high with newspapers. Seeing Dirk she squealed, 'Dirk, you're all right,' dropped the newspapers and threw her arms round the dragon's neck. Never having been hugged before Dirk wasn't sure how to react. He reached out his forepaw and awkwardly patted Holly's back. Sensing his embarrassment, Holly withdrew and knelt down to pick up the newspapers.

'I'm so glad you're OK,' she said. 'I was beginning to wonder if you'd ever wake up.'

'Why? How long have I been out?'

'Three days,' replied Holly.

Dirk crawled on all fours across the room and settled behind his desk. 'What happened to me?' he asked.

'Don't you remember?' replied Holly. 'You rescued the cats then you passed out.'

'The cats, yes, that's right. I swam out, something was holding on to the crate. I bit into it then it all went black.'

'What do you mean, something was holding on to it? Like what?' asked Holly.

'I don't know, but whatever it was tasted pretty bad. Was your cat in the crate?'

'Yes, you saved Willow. Thank you so much. She

means more to me than anything. I can pay you. I've got some money saved.'

'That's great, kiddo, but right now I'm more interested in how I got myself across London unconscious? That sounds pretty impressive even for me.'

'I got Mrs Klingerflim to come and pick us up.'

'Mrs Klingerflim . . .' started Dirk anxiously.

'Don't worry. She doesn't know,' interrupted Holly. 'She really is blind. The scariest roller coaster in the world has nothing on a short road trip with that woman. I told her you were ill and she gave me this home-made medicine.' Holly held up a bottle of distinctly dubious-looking brown liquid and handed it to Dirk.

Dirk opened the bottle and sniffed cautiously.

'Apparently it used to work wonders on her poor Ivor,' said Holly.

Dirk lifted it to his mouth and sipped. It tasted revolting, like boiled cabbage and sewage.

'Eurgh!' he said. 'It's no wonder the poor man died.'

Holly laughed.

'Well,' he said, putting the bottle down. 'I guess I owe you one. Thanks. But, if you've got your cat then the case is closed. Why are you still around?'

‘Closed? It’s far from closed. Look at these.’ She slammed the pile of the papers on the desk between them.

Dirk reached out a paw, twisted the top paper round and read out loud, ‘“Allotment owners complain of stolen vegetables. ‘It’s a case of bean and gone,’ said allotment owner, Len Cooper”’

‘The story above that,’ said Holly impatiently.

Dirk read:

CAT-ASTROPHE
Police flummoxed by the mass disappearance of pet cats in London.

The second paper read:

CAT BURGLARS STRIKE AGAIN
Londoners board up their cat flaps
as cat theft increases by 340%.

And another:

CAT-CH ME IF YOU CAN
Cat thieves continue to evade the authorities as more moggies go missing.

'We rescued those cats, but there's loads more still missing. I heard those two crooks say it was their fourth time down to the river. What's happened to the poor cats in the other three crates? What are they doing with them?'

'I don't know,' replied Dirk. 'Have you gone to the police?'

'The police? No way. This is our case,' replied Holly. 'Look, I'll tell you what I've found out . . .'

'No,' interrupted Dirk, remembering the resolution he had made while swimming in the Thames. 'This isn't our case. It's my case. Don't get me wrong, I'm grateful, kiddo, I really am . . .'

'What? For saving your life?'

'Yeah, for that,' said Dirk. 'But I can't let you get involved. You're only a kid and you're only a human. I suggest you go home, board up your cat flap and hold on to Willow, but this isn't your case any more.'

Holly stared angrily at Dirk. 'Not my case? If it wasn't for me you'd still be lying by the Thames or possibly in it.'

'It's for your own good.'

'How do you know anything about my own good?' Holly stared intently into his large, yellow eyes.

Dirk glanced around his office. There was something odd about it. It took him a moment to work out what. It was tidy. In fact, it was more than tidy. It was clean. All the empty baked-bean tins and bottles of orange squash had been thrown away, the newspapers piled neatly into a corner and the details of previous cases had been picked up and actually filed in the filing cabinet. The broken desk had been propped up on old phone directories. Tentatively he pulled open a desk drawer. The paperclips, pens and pencils had all been sorted into different colours. The drawer had even been lined with floral paper. He lowered his nose and sniffed. It was even worse than he had thought. It was scented paper.

'How much time have you spent here?' he asked.

'I've been here every day,' replied Holly, 'working on the case.'

'And what about school? What about your parents?'

'Oh, don't worry about them,' said Holly casually.

'And yet I find I am worried. Look, kiddo, I don't want any trouble and if you keep sneaking off here instead of going to school that's exactly what you'll attract.'

'My parents think I am going to school.'

'And what about your school?'

'They think I'm at home with the flu. I do an amazing impression of my dad's wife, if I do say so myself.'

'And they don't suspect a thing?'

'I've done it before. I've been to quite a few schools in my time. I know the systems.'

'How many schools?'

'One . . . two . . . three . . .' Holly counted out on her fingers. 'Four . . . five schools,' she announced proudly.

'Right,' said Dirk. 'And if you're so good at this, why do you keep getting expelled?'

'I wasn't expelled from all of them. The first one I had to leave because we moved down to London. Dad was working here a lot. He's a politician. He works in the Ministry of Defence, and his big-haired wife was worried that he might start playing up if left to his own devices. So we moved down to join him. That was the only school I liked.'

'But you were expelled from the other four?'

'Three. This is my fifth now. Anyway, they're bound to find out some time, but I've only just started this one, so I reckon I've got a good few months before either of them figure it out. Honestly, my parents don't really care what I do as long as I stay out of their way.'

'Listen, I'm not a child counsellor and I'm not an educational psychologist and if you want to mess up your own education and never learn to read or write . . .'

'I can read and write very well, thanks, and do maths and art and science and I'm teaching myself the trumpet. I just get my education from places other than school.'

'Again, you're confusing me with someone who gives a rat's bandana. I really don't care what you do with your life, but you're not getting involved with this case.'

Holly looked down and placed her head in her hands and began to wail, but Dirk instantly interrupted her. 'And don't think that's going to work again,' he said sternly.

Holly stopped dead, looked up, her eyes dry and clear, and said, 'I've got information.'

'What information?'

'Like who owns the warehouse.'

'The warehouse? How did you . . .'

'I told you, I get my education from places other than school. I heard those crooks talking about a Mr G. I did a little research and I think I know what the

G stands for.'

'And?'

'Are we partners, then?' asked Holly pulling out a piece of paper.

'Give me that,' said Dirk, reaching out to grab it. Holly whipped it away quickly.

'Partners?' she said, maintaining eye contact.

Dirk stared into the girl's brown eyes. He could easily take the paper from her by force, but it just didn't seem right. She had saved his life. She had been both brave and resourceful back at the river and now she had found a vital clue. And he was already too far behind with the case, having spent the last three days unconscious. He bowed his head and muttered, 'OK.'

'I'm sorry?' smiled Holly. 'I can't hear you?'

'OK,' said Dirk louder, 'but just this case. And you do what I say, all right?'

'Absolutely,' said Holly.

'And you're still the most annoying human I've ever met.'

Holly stretched out her spare hand and Dirk met her with his paw. They shook and, with a triumphant look upon her face, Holly passed over the document.

Chapter Twelve

Dirk grabbed the piece of paper and read. The property was owned by a Mr V. Grandin. The name rang a bell, but it wasn't a big bell like the one you heard before the news at ten. It was softer, like the sort of bell an old lady might have on a bicycle, quiet but persistent enough to nag at you.

'The warehouse is registered under the company name of Gronkong Shinard Plc,' said Holly. 'I checked your previous cases while I was filing them. You haven't got any record of a Gronkong Shinard. I called Company House, where they keep a record of all registered companies in the country, but they didn't have any other information on it. Grandin is also a bit of a mystery. He's not listed in the phone book. And there's no mention of him on the Internet.'

'Good research,' said Dirk, trying not to sound too impressed, 'But this case calls for some good old-fashioned groundwork.' He grabbed a large coat and hat from the hat stand behind the door. 'Sorry, kiddo, can't take you on this one.'

'But we're partners,' said Holly. 'That means doing everything together.'

'Sorry,' replied Dirk. 'There are some places I just can't take you.'

'That's fine,' said Holly, picking up a phone directory, opening it up and lifting the receiver.

'What are you doing?'

'Hiring a detective to follow you,' she replied, dialling a number.

Dirk whipped out his tail and knocked the phone off the table, yanking the receiver out of Holly's hand. It landed heavily on the floor.

Holly pulled out some change from her pocket. 'I'll just go and use the phone box,' she said.

Dirk scowled at her. He growled at her. Black smoke billowed from his nostrils but the brown-haired, brown-eyed girl just smiled back at him defiantly. He looked away in frustration then up in thought. The trail of smoke from his nose turned light grey and took shape, forming into a dragon's head.

'I guess as long as no one else sees her . . .' Dirk muttered to himself. 'The Shade-Hugger isn't stupid enough to say anything . . . not with everything that I've got on him . . .' The smoke dragon dissipated and Dirk said to Holly, 'All right, but it's at your own risk.'

Holly put the phone back on the desk. 'Great,' she said, grinning.

Dirk looked at the clock. The big hand was pointing to the right, the small hand, downwards. He scratched his head.

'It's a quarter past six,' said Holly helpfully.

'I knew that,' he snapped. 'Here,' he said, throwing the hat and coat at Holly.

'Why do I need these?' she asked, catching them.

'They're not for you. Come on, let's go.'

'Hold on,' said Holly and she opened a carton of milk and poured it into a bowl in the corner of the room. A cat miaowed and Willow appeared from under the table.

'Why is there a cat in my office?' asked Dirk coldly.

'She's safer here,' replied Holly. 'You wouldn't want her to get stolen again, would you?'

Dirk groaned. 'As long as she doesn't *do* anything,' he said, eyeing the animal suspiciously.

'What, like mess up the place?' laughed Holly. 'I don't think you need any help with that.'

Dirk pulled up the blind and checked the street. A grey Mercedes with a white stripe was parked illegally on the double-yellow lines. Next to it stood a man in a long raincoat and a wide-brimmed hat. He looked up and Dirk backed away from the window. One of the reasons he liked the spot was the fact that cars couldn't park below. It lessened the chances of being seen jumping out of the window. Luckily the traffic wardens were a voracious lot and no one ever got away with it for long. Sure enough, after a moment Dirk saw two of them hurrying towards the car. The man in the long coat dived into the car and drove away, leaving the disappointed traffic wardens to head off in search of their next victim.

'Come on, let's go,' said Dirk.

'Are we going back to the warehouse?' asked Holly.

'No. Here, hold these.' And he grabbed a couple of bags of assorted liquorice sweets and handed them to Holly. She stuffed them in her pockets and climbed on to his large, red back, carefully positioning the hat and coat between her and the dragon.

Dirk pushed open the window, glanced down again and then leapt on to the neighbouring roof.

Bathed in the reddish glow from the setting sun, the rooftops of London looked even more magical to Holly this evening. She was doing her best to think tough like a proper detective, but looking down at the yellow lamps and the people below going about their humdrum lives, unaware of the dragon leaping over their heads, she couldn't help but feel excited and special.

Dirk decided it was time to tell Holly about the catnapping dragons he had witnessed. As they travelled, he described how he had followed the Mountain Dragon to the warehouse and then narrowly avoided being seen by the Sea Dragon shortly afterwards.

'Wow, so there are loads of dragons in London,' said Holly. 'What do you think they're doing with the cats?' she asked. 'You don't think they're eating them, do you?'

'Not likely,' replied Dirk. 'Unlike humans, dragons don't eat other animals,'

'Not all humans. I'm a vegetarian too,' said Holly.

'You choose not to eat meat. For us it's death to

consume the body of another living creature.'

Holly looked around at their surroundings. She was lost. 'Where are we?' she asked.

'We're in Greenwich,' replied Dirk.

'What's in Greenwich?'

'Well, there's a nice market, a naval college, a couple of good pubs and a lovely park,' joked Dirk.

'I mean, what's in Greenwich for us?'

'The underground.'

'We're getting the tube?'

'Something like that,' replied Dirk and he jumped on to a large clock tower and scampered up its side, gaining enough height to spread his wings and glide down on to a row of houses. He ran across the houses then sailed over a glass-topped market place. One more jump and he landed on a flat pub roof next to a concrete concourse beside the River Thames. Holly stopped herself from squealing with excitement like she was on the best roller-coaster ride in the world ever.

She dismounted and looked down. In the middle of the concourse was an old tall ship that she remembered was called the *Cutty Sark* and by its side a cylindrical concrete structure with a green dome-like top.

'That's the entrance to the pedestrian tunnel under the Thames,' said Dirk, pointing to the structure.

'I know,' replied Holly. 'I came here on a school trip once.'

'*You* went on a school trip?' said Dirk disbelievingly.

'It wasn't my school. I'd had an argument with my dad's wife, so I ran away and then I saw a coach and just jumped on it. It turned out to be a school trip, so I pretended I went to their school.'

Dirk laughed, 'You're growing on me, kiddo. Now, give me the hat and coat.'

Holly handed him the giant coat. Laughter rose up from the pub garden below. Someone dropped a glass. It smashed on the ground, receiving a round of applause and a drunken cheer.

Dirk pulled the coat over his shoulders, covering his wings. He tucked his long nose under his chin and buttoned it up. Next he put the hat over his head and pulled it down. He swished his tail twice and then curled it up behind him, making the coat taut and strangely shaped. He took a step back and said in a muffled voice, 'How do I look?'

Holly looked at him. Although he had succeeded in hiding his distinctive dragon features he still looked pretty bizarre. Even with his tail tucked in and his head bowed he was still taller than the average human adult. Then there were the large yellow eyes that glowed from under the wide-brimmed hat. Not to mention the bulges of his nose and tail, which made it look as though he suffered from terrible growths.

'This normally works, does it?' asked Holly doubtfully.

'Well, tell me,' muttered Dirk, 'do I look like the sort of person you want to strike up a conversation with?'

'No,' said Holly honestly.

'Then it works,' said Dirk. 'Come on.' He looked over the edge of the building and, sure that no one was looking, grabbed Holly round her waist and jumped down, landing heavily on the concrete ground without the use of his wings to ease the impact.

He put her down and they walked quickly to the tunnel entrance, moving with the shadows and avoiding eye contact with passing strangers. Dirk led them down a large spiral staircase that encircled the lift.

At the bottom they headed down the long tunnel

under the river. The lift opened behind them and a young couple got out.

Dirk slowed his pace. 'Let them overtake,' he muttered.

As the couple passed they glanced back at them and it occurred to Holly how strange they must look. She tried to act normally but it was difficult with the strange figure in the overcoat towering above her.

Dirk kept a slow pace and it wasn't long before the couple had disappeared round the corner. He stopped. 'Through this door,' he said.

'What door?' asked Holly.

Dirk pulled an old rusty key from his jacket pocket and pushed it into a hole in the wall, where it looked like a couple of tiles had fallen away. He turned the key and pushed the wall with his shoulder, revealing a door. 'In,' he said.

Holly looked into the darkness then entered. Dirk followed. He pulled the door shut, plunging them into darkness. He turned on a torch and handed it to her.

'Follow me,' he said, discarding the hat and coat and disappearing down the dark corridor.

Chapter Thirteen

The corridor was narrow and winding. Holly could hear their footsteps echoing and the continual swish of the river above them. She kept her eyes fixed on the small circle of light created by the torch, trying not to look into the darkness, where her imagination was able to summon up all manner of scary beasts. She didn't want Dirk to know that she was scared, so she made up a tune to the rhythm of her footsteps and whistled it to calm her down.

'Stop that,' said Dirk.

'Stop what?' asked Holly.

'Whistling. No whistling.'

Holly hummed the tune instead.

'Or humming,' snapped Dirk.

Holly stopped humming. For a moment she made no noise at all and then in a clear voice she sang the tune: 'La de da da da da daah.'

'Look, no music at all, OK,' said Dirk, turning round. His face was deadly serious.

'Don't you like music?' she asked.

'No, I don't.'

'Don't dragons have songs?'

'Oh yes, we have songs all right,' Dirk said grimly. 'But for dragons music isn't for fun. It's the deadliest weapon of all.'

'Oh,' said Holly. 'Remind me never to go to a dragon disco.'

'Very funny,' said Dirk stonily. 'Come on, there are some stairs, coming up.'

They continued walking until they came to the top of a flight of stairs, which they followed downwards. At the bottom was a small stone room. Holly followed Dirk in.

'Hold on to me,' he said. 'And don't be scared.'

She started to say that she wasn't scared but got as far as 'I'm not sc–' before she was cut short by a strange growling, muttering noise, syncopated by clicks and barks. Before she could ask what it was she realised that the noise was coming from Dirk. He was talking, but not in a language that she had ever heard before. This, she supposed, was Dragonspeak. Before she could begin to wonder whom he might be talking to, she felt her stomach lurch. The room was moving downwards. She grabbed on to Dirk and shone the torch at the doorway. The stairs had vanished, replaced by a solid stone wall, rushing past.

'It's a lift,' she said.

'Of sorts, yes,' replied Dirk, as the room took them deeper and deeper into the bowels of the earth.

'Where will it take us?'

'To Karnataka.'

'What's Karnataka?' The constant motion of the lift was making her feel sick.

'Who, not what.'

'Who's Karnataka, then?'

'Well, until a few days ago Karnataka was the only other London-based dragon that I was aware of. Only he lives deep down here, underneath the city. He's a Shade-Hugger. They're not big fans of sunlight.'

'And why are we going to see him?'

'Because he doesn't just keep his ear to the ground.

Karnataka lives in the ground. If an earthworm wriggles in Ealing, Karnataka knows about it.'

The room stopped moving. Holly pointed the torch out of the doorway and saw that they had arrived at a large dimly lit tunnel in front of a giant door carved in the shape of a dragon's head, with a huge ring through its nose. The air tasted stale and humid, and lacking in oxygen. She followed Dirk out of the lift towards the door. He jumped up, grabbed the huge metal ring between his teeth, pulled it back and let it go. The bang reverberated off the rocks, echoing seemingly for ever into the darkness. With a painful creak the door edged open. Dirk entered, followed by Holly, desperately trying to feel brave.

On the other side of the door was a great hall. Along each side were giant stone pillars, carved into the shapes of various creatures, each one more terrible and ferocious looking than the last. Some were dragons, like Dirk, others more serpent than dragon, or strange half-breeds like a cockerel crossed with a snake, or half cockroach, half vulture. Each figure sat upright with its mouth wide open, and from each mouth a constant jet of bright-red fire lit the great hall.

'Wow,' said Holly. 'Karnataka must be fairly important to live here.'

'You're confusing important with ostentatious,' replied Dirk.

'What does ostentatious mean?' asked Holly.

'He's a show-off,' said Dirk.

The fire from the pillars died away and an orotund voice spoke, each syllable emphasised by a burst of flame from the statues' mouths. 'Who dares enter the hall of Karnataka?'

'It's me, Dirk Dilly,' Dirk replied.

'And what does Dirk Dilly want that he dares to disturb the great Karnataka at his humble home?'

Holly stared into the darkness. Two large, red eyes watched them.

'Information,' said Dirk.

'And what payment do you have for me?' said the eyes.

Dirk pointed at Holly. 'I bring the sweetest human produce of all,' he said.

The lights dimmed then went out completely. Holly looked desperately at Dirk but it was too dark to see his face. The room was filled with the sound of echoing footsteps, charging towards her. Holly turned to run, but felt a great weight land heavily on her back. She fell forwards.

'Get off me, get off me,' she yelled, kicking and screaming. 'I'm not your payment.'

'Payment?' said a high nasal voice. 'Just give us the liquorice and no one will get hurt.'

Holly felt something reach in her pockets and pull out the bags of liquorice that Dirk had given her earlier, and she was free again. She jumped to her feet and the lights flared up, revealing a dragon with a dark-brown back and caramel-coloured underbelly, greedily throwing the sweets into its mouth and munching happily.

'Sorry,' said Dirk to Holly. 'Karny likes his grand introductions.'

'You could have warned me,' said Holly. 'I thought he was going to eat me.'

'I keep telling you, dragons don't eat meat.'

'Yes, but . . .'

Karnataka looked up from his sweets. 'What are you doing bringing a human down here, Dirk?' He said in a nasal whine. 'You've finally lost it. You know the rules. You know what would happen. You're risking enough with all that detective nonsense as it is. If you're not careful, you'll be sent down.'

'What happened to your voice?' asked Holly.

'Oh, that?' said Karnataka, 'That's just a voice-echo device. It's good for scaring away unwanted intruders. That and the red-eye projector. You like the flames? The flames are new,' he added excitedly.

'Oh yes,' said Holly. 'I thought the flames were terrific. Really scary.'

'You see,' said Karnataka to Dirk. 'I told you the flames were worth it. Scary, she said.'

'I didn't come down here to discuss your Wizard of Oz complex, Karny. I came here for information.'

'Sure thing,' said Karnataka, throwing the last of the liquorice sweets up in the air and catching it in his mouth. 'That stuff really is the best. What can I do for you? Just name it. You have me at your disposal.'

'What have you got on a V. Grandin?'

Holly had never seen a face lose so much colour in so little time. Karnataka's yellow eyes whitened and he looked furtively from side to side as though suddenly scared that they were being watched.

'I'm . . . s . . . s . . . sorry,' stammered the dragon. 'I've never heard of no one of that name. Sorry I can't be more help, though and thanks for the liquorice.' He turned around and ran back into the darkness.

Holly and Dirk looked at each other.

'Bingo,' said Dirk and he walked slowly forwards.

Chapter Fourteen

'Come on, Karny,' Dirk called into the darkness. 'Play the game. You got your liquorice.'

Once again the large red eyes appeared and the deep voice echoed around the hall.

'The great dragon Karnataka is not in at the moment,' it said. 'But please leave a message after the tone and he'll be sure to get back to you. Beeep!'

'Karny.' There was a taunting quality to Dirk's voice. 'You can't hide from me.'

Holly walked by Dirk's side. They approached the eyes. She had stopped being scared of them now as she could see that they were in fact two red lights attached to something that looked like a giant ear trumpet.

'Karnataka forbids you to take one step further,' said the voice, with a hint of panic.

Dirk winked at Holly and walked around the strange device. Behind it was Karnataka, shaking with terror.

'You are trespassing,' boomed his voice. 'Trespass not against me or I–'

'Boo,' said Dirk in Karnataka's ear, causing the dragon to jump a metre in the air.

'Leave me alone,' he said in his normal high-pitched voice.

'Come on,' said Dirk. 'Do I have to force you?'

'Dirk. I can't. I don't know anything.'

'Is that right?' said Dirk. 'Then let's change the subject. How about . . . say, the Dragon Council's Welsh gold reserves. Know anything about them?'

A fresh look of panic crossed Karnataka's face. 'You wouldn't,' he said. 'You can't prove anything.'

'The Council aren't too fussy about proof. Remember what happened to poor Elsinor?'

'You leave my brother out of this.'

'They didn't have much proof on him, did they? And I'm sure they'd be interested to know how you can afford all these trinkets,' Dirk said, pointing at the rows of giant sculptures.

'All right,' said Karnataka, bowing his head in defeat. 'But not in front of the human.'

'She's with me,' said Dirk. 'Whatever you have to say to me you can say in front of her.'

'But you know the rules.'

'Since when have you cared so much about the rules?' Dirk challenged.

'Stealing a bit of gold is one thing, but breaching the forbidden divide is . . . well, it's just silly.'

Dirk bristled. 'Don't call me silly,' he snarled. 'She's only a kid. She doesn't really count. Just tell me what you know.'

'All right,' said Karnataka, walking along the hallway. Dirk and Holly followed. He stopped between a statue of a two-headed serpent and one of a giant snake-like creature with the head of a lion and two enormous wings. He turned around and in a low whisper uttered the words, 'Vainclaw Grandin.'

'Should I know him?' asked Dirk.

'It's better if you don't. It's safer if you don't. Vainclaw is a Mountain Dragon, like yourself. Only bigger, older and a whole lot meaner.'

'I can be pretty mean,' said Dirk.

'Don't I know it? But you don't even come close to Vainclaw. They say he drinks the blood of other dragons in order to steal their powers. This is the dragon that testified against Minertia and made sure that she was banished to the Inner Core. Get in his way, you're dragon ash. I hear rumours all the time, but his name is always whispered. They say he's got followers too.'

'Followers?' said Dirk.

Karnataka glanced around again and said, 'They call him the first up-airer, Dirk.'

'You're not suggesting that he's planning–'

'I don't know.' Karnataka interrupted him. 'But you know what he's calling his followers? The Kinghorns. They're back, Dirk. They're back.'

'They've got something in the Thames. Any idea what?'

'Like what?'

'Something nasty. Something you bite into it, it knocks you out.'

'I'll do some digging,' replied Karnataka.

'Do that,' said Dirk. 'I'll bring the liquorice.'

'Thanks. Don't worry about the coconut ones next time. They give me terrible wind.'

Dirk turned to Holly and said, 'It's time we left.' He thanked Karnataka for the information and told him what would happen if he mentioned seeing Dirk with a human to anyone – which involved a mouthful of fire and the softer, squidgier parts of Karnataka's anatomy.

Holly said goodbye to the dragon and they exited through the great doors, which shut very quickly behind them. They entered the small room and Dirk made a strange noise again, which caused the lift to make its way back up towards the surface.

Making his way across the roofs of London with Holly on his back, under the purple night sky, Dirk said, 'We need to get you home. Your parents will be worried.'

'They think I'm in my room. I left the radio on and dad's wife knows not to enter my room without my permission.'

'Still, it's getting late,' said Dirk.

Under the cover of darkness Dirk travelled quickly and it wasn't long before he was perched on the roof across the street from Holly's house.

'You think it's a dragon in the Thames?' asked Holly.

'There are bigger, scarier and older things than dragons in the world,' replied Dirk. 'I don't know what they've got.'

'And what's an up-airer? Who are the Kinghorns? Who is Minertia?' asked Holly.

'Tomorrow,' replied Dirk. 'It's late and it's a long story.'

'Shall I come to the office?' asked Holly.

'You should be at school. They'll get suspicious.'

'They'll get more suspicious if I do turn up. Tomorrow's Saturday.'

'OK, then. Come to the office at that time when both hands are pointing up.'

'Twelve o'clock?'

'That's the one. And bring something warm to wear and binoculars if you have them.'

'OK. I'll borrow my dad's.'

Dirk jumped to Holly's roof. A voice on the radio said, ' . . . We're talking about the ongoing mystery of the missing cats. Where do you think they have gone?'

'Is that your window below us?' Dirk asked.

'Yes,' replied Holly.

'Hang on,' he said, flapping his wings, lifting them both off the roof and lowering them down level with

Holly's open window. Dirk backed up a little and Holly climbed into the room.

'See you tomorrow,' she said. 'Remember to feed Willow. Her food is in the bottom desk drawer.'

'Like I have any choice,' said Dirk and he flew back to the safety of the roof.

The DJ was saying, 'One man with a theory is behavioural animal psychologist Dr Gustav Gunter. And Dr Gunter joins us now.'

'Hello, Peter,' said a second voice. 'As you know I have dedicated my life to ze scientific study of ze feline form and have known for many years ze truth zat cats are in fact alien beings from outer space sent to spy on us. Zey are simply going home now.'

'Fascinating. Spy on us for what reason, Dr Gunter?'

'I do not know. Zey may have been sent by a giant master cat planning on attacking earth. However, zis is mere speculation. We cannot be sure as to their motives.'

'Right, a giant master cat, eh? I wonder what colour it would be?'

'Most likely, it would be a ginger cat,' replied the doctor.

Dirk headed back to the office, where he sat by the

window, knocking back orange squash on the rocks, blowing smoke shapes and reluctantly stroking the cat until he fell asleep with Willow sleeping on his soft, green belly.

Chapter Fifteen

The next day, Dirk and Holly travelled across the city's rooftops, under a grey and featureless sky.

'Are we going back to the warehouse?' asked Holly.

'No,' replied Dirk. 'Today we're going to find out exactly how many dragons we're up against.'

'How do we do that?'

Dirk stopped. They were in the area known as Docklands. Holly's dad sometimes had meetings here with important businessmen or influential newspaper editors. She had heard him say that many years ago the area had been used for packing goods on to ships and exporting them around the world. These days it had become a centre of business and home to the highest buildings in London.

Dirk looked up. Holly followed his gaze. Towering above them was an enormous office block.

'Up there,' he replied.

On weekdays the area was full of business types in expensive suits. They poured out of the trains in the morning and back on again at the end of the working day. Today, a Saturday, it was less hectic, but there were still plenty of people milling around the shops and restaurants or just enjoying a walk by the still dock waters.

Dirk perched on the tip of a flat-topped office building and looked up at the skyscraper in front of him.

'How are we getting up there?' asked Holly.

'With these,' he replied, flapping his wings. 'Come on, I'd better hold you.'

Holly slid off the dragon's back and he grabbed her, holding her securely against his belly.

'Won't we be seen?' she asked. 'It's a long way and there are a lot of people down there. Someone's bound to look up.'

'Ever heard of a smokescreen?' said Dirk. He cleared his throat and snorted. Grey smoke billowed from his nostrils. Holly shut her eyes tight to keep the smoke out. Dirk spun round on the spot a couple of times, still snorting, until the smoke completely enveloped them. He flapped his wings and Holly felt her feet lifted off the roof.

On the ground below, a married couple sat on a bench, eating supermarket sandwiches in silence. The husband looked up at the cloud of smoke rising above the buildings. 'Now, there's a peculiar thing,' he said, accidentally spitting a bit of sandwich at his wife.

'Don't speak with your mouth full,' said his wife irritably.

'It looks like a big smoke signal,' he continued. 'I saw a documentary about Native Americans once. It said smoke signals were like an early form of mobile phone call.'

'Pah,' said his wife. 'What can you say with smoke signals?'

'Useful things like "Danger" and "All's Well".'

'What if you want to say something more complicated like, "If you loved me you'd buy me the Bobby Smoo shoes that I wanted."'

'Are you still going on about those flipping shoes?' said the husband. 'We could buy a flat-screen TV for the same price.'

And so they had an argument and forgot all about the strange clump of smoke that was now level with the top of the building.

Dirk touched down on top of the skyscraper and the smoke dissipated to reveal a breathtaking view of the city. He located the warehouse and pointed it out to Holly, who found it with her binoculars.

'What am I looking for?' she asked.

'Dragons,' replied Dirk.

Holly saw something grey emerge from the warehouse and jump to the next building. It moved quickly and she wouldn't have spotted it at all if she hadn't known where to look. 'I can see one,' she said.

'Yes, that's our Sea Dragon friend. That's one. Let's see where he goes.'

Following it with her binoculars she said, 'So are you going to fill me in or what?'

Dirk looked at Holly. She knew so much already, he decided he may as well give her the full picture. It was against every rule in the book, but what were rules for if not to be broken?

'Dragons have been around for a long time,' he said. 'Since before the dinosaurs.'

'You were around the same time as dinosaurs?' she replied.

'Me? Do I look that old to you? No, I wasn't, but there are dragons old enough to remember them. Of course, the dinosaurs died out and there came a new species, smaller but even more deadly. It called itself mankind. For thousands of years dragons and man lived side by side. Men were too scared of the big teeth and the whole fire caboodle to cause any trouble, but over time they made themselves weapons and they got less scared and they developed a taste for dragon blood. It became like a sport for them. With every passing year they got cleverer and their weapons became more sophisticated. It was clear that the planet was no longer big enough to share. Look, there's another one.' Dirk pointed at a second dragon jumping across London. 'Looks like a yellow-backed Scavenger. Best avoided.'

Holly peered carefully at the dragon. 'Why?' she asked. 'Are they dangerous?'

'Dangerous, yes, but bad breath too. Pooh!' Dirk held his nose and Holly laughed. 'Look, there are two of them,' he said.

Sure enough, there were two yellow-backed dragons moving in opposite directions.

'Dragons were fighting back,' continued Dirk. 'The world was on the brink of a full-scale war. Something had to be done. So Minertia, the greatest and oldest dragon of them all, called a conference high in the Himalayas. All of dragonkind came: Sea Dragons, Mountain Dragons, Tree Dragons, Snow Dragons, Desert Dragons, even Sky Dragons, yellow-backed Scavengers, pot-bellied Cave Dwellers, Shade-Huggers, Drakes, Wyverns, you name it, they came and spread themselves over the mountains as far as the eye could see.'

'Were you there?' asked Holly.

'Yes, but I was very young. I remember Minertia, as big as a mountain herself, flying over and explaining that we had a choice. The biggest decision in our long history. Either we could eradicate mankind before their weapons got too powerful or we could bide our time, go into hiding until mankind went the way of the dinosaurs. It was put to the vote. Those in favour of fighting rose into the air. Those who wanted to hide stayed on the ground. Minertia counted the vote and announced that it had been decided that dragonkind would hide and let the human race run its course.'

'So an up-airer is a dragon that wanted to go to

war?' said Holly.

'Exactly, and it sounds like this Vainclaw dragon is claiming to be the first one in the air, which is impossible to prove, of course.'

'What did you do?'

'I stayed on the ground. Look, another.' Dirk pointed down at a fourth dragon.

Holly found it with the binoculars. 'It looks like you,' she said.

'Yes, it's the Mountain Dragon that I saw around your house. It's probably the one that picked up your cat.'

Holly watched the dragon head south, and asked, 'So what's a Kinghorn?'

'Well, before the great vote, a group of dragons calling themselves the Kinghorns organised attacks on human settlements. They were cowardly, mostly targeting the women and children of villages that didn't have armies or knights to defend them. They wanted to end mankind's reign before it started. The Kinghorns were all up-airers. After the vote the attacks were outlawed by the Dragon Council. Anyone found guilty of attacking humans was banished to the Inner Core.'

Holly said, 'So if Vainclaw is calling his followers

the Kinghorns it means . . .'

'Trouble,' said Dirk.

For another hour or so, they stayed watching the dragons jumping across the roofs of London. Holly grew cold and huddled close to Dirk's belly for warmth.

Eventually Dirk stood up and said, 'Well, this is good news.'

'What do you mean good news? There's a group of dragons in London planning to wipe out the human race,' exclaimed Holly. 'What's good about it?'

'Well, they don't even know that we're on to them, but we know where they're hiding, what they're doing, and that there are only four of them.'

Chapter Sixteen

Back in Dirk's office, Holly stroked Willow and asked, 'So what next?'

Dirk sat, feet on the desk, flicking through the collections of cat puns that constituted the day's front pages.

'I'm going to get into that warehouse and get to the bottom of this,' he replied, putting the papers down on the desk.

'Great,' said Holly, spinning round on the chair, causing Willow to let out a distressed miaow and dig her claws into her lap. 'Ow,' she said, pulling the cat off and putting her down on the floor. 'How do we get in?'

'Not we,' said the dragon. '*I* am going in. We're dealing with four genuine fire-breathing dragons intent on eradicating mankind. It's too dangerous for you. And don't even start with the pretend-crying again. It may work on your parents but . . .'

'I don't use it on my parents,' Holly interjected angrily.

'Well, you want to watch that. One day you'll be crying for real and no one will care because they'll think you're faking,' said Dirk.

'I don't cry for real,' she replied. 'And this is our case. You said so. I saved your life.'

'And now I'm saving yours.' He stood up and peaked through the blinds at the street below. 'Rats,' he said, standing back away from the window.

'What is it?' asked Holly.

'It's that man again. He was there before. He's watching the place.' Holly jumped up and looked out of the window. Leaning against a lamp-post across the road was a man wearing a wide-brimmed hat. 'You think they're on to us?' she said.

'Could be. There aren't many dragons who know about me, but if you know who to ask . . .'

'And you have enough liquorice,' added Holly.

'Exactly,' said Dirk, smiling. 'And we know that this

Vainclaw character isn't above hiring humans to do his dirty work.'

Holly thought for a moment and then said, 'I'll go and distract him.'

'No, we don't know what these people are capable of,' Dirk replied.

'Don't worry. I'll take Mrs Klingerflim. They wouldn't do anything in front of a little old lady.'

'What will you tell her?'

'I'll just say that we're playing a joke on an old friend of yours.'

Unable to think of a better plan Dirk said, 'OK, but be careful,' before adding quietly, 'And thanks.'

'But I want a full report of what you find out,' said Holly.

'Yes, sir,' said Dirk with a mock salute.

'At ease,' responded Holly and, with a smile, she left the room. Dirk heard her call Mrs Klingerflim as she thudded downstairs. He didn't hear what she said to her, but after a couple of minutes the front door slammed shut. Peeking through the blinds, Dirk saw Holly and Mrs Klingerflim leave the building. On the opposite side of the road stood the man in the wide-brimmed hat. Dirk edged the window open a little to hear what was going on.

'Excuse me, sir,' he heard Holly shout.

The man didn't reply, suddenly becoming very interested in his own shoes.

'Excuse me,' she repeated. 'Can you help this elderly lady across this road? She can't see very well and I'm too young to be crossing the road myself, but she needs to go to the post office to collect her pension.'

The man glanced up at the window for a second, then turned round and walked away as quickly as his feet could carry him.

'Good work, kiddo,' said Dirk under his breath. He pulled up the blind, thrust the window open and jumped out. As he flew over the road he caught a fleeting glimpse of Holly looking up and smiling.

The streets surrounding the warehouse were deserted and Dirk stood in the shadow of a nearby building. Going through the roof was too risky with the dragons constantly going in and out. If he was going to get in he would have to enter the way the humans did. Through the door.

Checking that no one was around he scuttled across the road to the barbed-wire fence, where the gate was secured with an enormous chain, held in place by a huge padlock. *Not a problem*, he thought and opened his mouth, put the chain between his teeth and slammed his jaw shut, biting straight through it.

'Pah,' he said, spitting bits of metal out of his mouth and slipping into the yard. *So far so good*, he thought. Looking around he could see the pile of drainpiping that he had ripped off the wall. The caravan and the old once-white van sat deserted in opposite corners. Cautiously he approached the door to the warehouse.

He pushed the door, but it was locked. He examined it closely. Some locks he could pick with a claw, but this was a Yale. Too small. He walked around the building, but there were no windows. There was only one thing for it. He was going to have to shoulder the door. He stepped back to make a run up and was about to charge when he heard the sound of a toilet flushing, followed by a CLICK. He turned to see the caravan door opening. He dived behind the once-white van just as the door opened fully, and heard a voice.

'You, Reginald, are an animal. An animal.'

'It's only natural, ain't it, Arthur?'

It was the two crooks.

'There is nothing natural about that smell. In fact,

I would go so far as to call it supernatural. Out of this world. And I thought we agreed that the mobile-home facilities would be exclusively utilised for the act of micturation,' said the tall, pompous man.

'Eh?'

'No pooing in the caravan toilet.'

Dirk raised his head so he could see the two men.

'Sorry, Arthur, it was that curry I had last night.'

'Much as I would dearly love to stand here discussing your bowel movements, we have more pressing duties.'

'Oh yeah,' said Reg, scratching his head. 'I'm not sure this is right. I mean cats is one thing . . .'

'Thank you for your opinion, Reg,' interrupted Arthur. 'And as fascinating as this lecture on the morality of criminality is no doubt going to be, could you please save it for after we have finished the assigned duties and been remunerated for our efforts.'

'No, you've lost me again.'

'Oh, never mind. Come on.'

Dirk ducked. They were not walking towards the warehouse. They were heading for the van.

He looked around desperately, but there was nowhere to hide. He edged round the back of the vehicle and pulled at the doors, but they were locked shut. The crooks were getting nearer. In a second they would see him. The two men continued bickering, their voices growing louder and louder as they grew closer.

And then he heard a third voice, that of a young girl. 'Ex . . . excuse me.' She sounded upset. 'I've lost my mummy and I don't know where I am.'

The two men stopped and turned in their tracks. Dirk looked through the van window. On the other side of the fence, standing on the pavement, rubbing her eyes, was Holly.

The short, fat man walked towards her. 'Don't cry,' he said.

'I'm sorry. I just need some money, so I can phone my mummy,' she continued in what was proving to be an Oscar-winning performance.

'I don't think we can help,' said the taller man coldly.

'Oh, don't be so mean. She's just a little girl, all alone,' said the other. To Holly he said, 'I'll get you some money, little girl. Hold on.' And he disappeared into the caravan.

'Stay here,' added Arthur, following Reg in.

'Go,' said Holly in an urgent whisper.

Dirk emerged from behind the van.

'Quick,' she said. 'They'll be out any second.'

'Thanks,' said Dirk. 'Looks like I owe you again. Now you get out of here too. Those two may be stupid, but they're still dangerous.'

'Mrs Klingerflim gave me a lift,' said Holly. 'You don't know danger till you've been in a car with that woman. Go!'

Dirk nodded, braced himself and ran at the warehouse door, which easily gave way. He shut the door behind him and looked around at the four large wooden crates with the words **DO NOT OPEN** written on the outside. Dirk noticed that there were air holes in them.

And then a bell rang.

'Ratingdon Ratstein the third,' he swore.

He knew what the bell meant.

Company.

Chapter Seventeen

The bell rang again and the lids of the four large wooden crates slowly rose. It was like something out of a tacky vampire movie Dirk had once sat up watching. But these weren't plywood coffins containing bit actors wearing too much make-up. From the claws that were pushing open the crates he knew that these were dragons. And they were real. Very real.

He dived over a crate, somersaulted mid-air, spread his wings and flew up into the shadows. He grabbed on to a rafter and blended with the wall, as the four large crates burst open, the lids clattering to the floor. Out crawled four dragons: the Mountain and the Sea

Dragon, and the two yellow-backed Scavengers. Dirk held his breath. The dragons prowled towards the centre of the warehouse.

The larger of the two Scavengers raised his head and said in barking, clicking Dragonspeak, 'Brothers Kinghorn, Dragons true, In the name of Vainclaw, I greet you.'

The red Mountain Dragon and the grey Sea Dragon bowed and said together, 'Dragons be free, Vainclaw we obey, save no mercy, for those who stand in our way.'

The smaller Scavenger said nothing.

'Speak the words, Mali?' said the larger of the two in English.

'Speak the words, Mali,' mimicked the smaller.

'Say it,' demanded the other, squaring up to fight.

'Leave it out, bro. I ain't saying that twaddle. Who talks like that, anyway, eh? It's bad enough having to hide in these poxy boxes all day, as it is,' he said petulantly.

'Look, if you don't want to be a Kinghorn, ar' kid, then you can just run back to Mummy and . . .'

'Leave Ma out of this, Leon,' snarled the dragon.

'You know you were adopted, don't you, eh, Mali?' goaded the larger.

'I was not.'

'Mum told me she found you under a blueberry bush while she was out picking berries.'

'She did not.'

'Blueberry boy!'

'Shut up.'

The two yellow-backed dragons were standing nose to nose, smoke billowing from their nostrils, cicling angrily.

The Sea Dragon edged himself between them and pushed them away from each other.

'Can you two cut it out?' he said. 'This mission's bad enough as it is without you two fighting like cats and . . . ah ah . . . ' He tipped his head back and then a giant sneeze roared from his mouth. 'Choo!' he screamed, sending a line of fire across the room, catching the Mountain Dragon's rear.

The Mountain Dragon yelped. 'Leave it out, Flotsam,' he said.

'Sorry, Jegsy,' said the Sea Dragon. 'It's these flipping cat hairs. They get everywhere. I picked up a white Persian this morning and it's really making me . . . ah . . . ah . . . ahh . . . CHOO!'

Another line of fire darted out. This time the Mountain Dragon jumped out of the way.

Unfortunately he wasn't looking where he was going and landed on the nose of the Scavenger called Mali.

'Ow, watch it!' said the Scavenger.

'Stop messing around, you idiots,' said his brother, Leon. 'We've got work to do.'

'And who appointed you leader, anyway?' demanded Mali.

'Vainclaw did when he personally asked me to make sure the mission went ahead without any hic-cups,' replied Leon, the larger of the Scavengers. 'Or sneezes,' he added, looking witheringly at Flotsam, the Sea Dragon.

'I think I should be in charge,' replied Mali, 'or Jegsy. He's Vainclaw's nephew.'

'No, I'm not bothered, like,' said Jegsy.

'Look, it's not important,' said Flotsam. 'I'll just be glad when I don't have to touch another flipping cah . . . ah . . . ah . . . CHOOOO.'

This time the two yellows dived out of the way of the fire, but collided with each other. *That's got to hurt*, thought Dirk, up in the rafters, as the two drag-ons' heads smacked together.

'You clumsy fool,' said Leon, rubbing his head.

'You ran into me,' growled Mali.

'Here, I've got just the thing for headaches, like,'

said the Mountain Dragon, Jegsy, and he dived into his crate. After a moment's rummaging he emerged holding what looked to Dirk like a child's yo-yo.

'What's that?' asked Flotsam.

'Well, I'm not sure, but I think it works like this,' replied Jegsy, threading the string through a claw. 'Stand still,' he said to Leon and, taking aim very carefully, he threw the yo-yo at Leon's head.

'Ouch,' snarled Leon angrily. 'What d'you think you're doing?'

'Oh, maybe that's not the right thing. Hold on.' He jumped back into the crate.

'Eh, you been on the rob again, Jegsy?' said Flotsam.

'It ain't robbing, like. I'm collecting,' said the Mountain Dragon, emerging from the crate holding a tennis racket, a plant pot and a large pair of rather grey-looking underpants.

'Vainclaw said we shouldn't take anything except for cats,' said Leon.

'Yeah, but he wouldn't mind the odd thing, like. It's so interesting, all this stuff. And I'm making real progress at understanding how it all works, ain't I? Right, try this.' He placed the plant pot on Leon's head, draped the pants over his nose and then began repeatedly hitting the plant pot with the tennis racket. 'How's that?' he asked.

'GET OFF ME, YOU IDIOT!' yelled Leon, shaking his head so that the plant pot smashed against a wall and sending the Y-fronts flying up in the air. The large yellow dragon threw his head back and roared. An enormous flame shot out of his mouth, burning the Y-fronts to a crisp and slightly singeing Dirk's behind. He swallowed the pain, knowing that the slightest movement would cause his skin to resume its natural colour, revealing him to the other dragons. Below, the charred remains of the pants rained down on the four dragons.

'Listen to me, you lot,' said Leon. 'Vainclaw doesn't want any unnecessary risks taken. This is too important.'

'Sorry, Leon.' Jegsy carefully dropped the tennis racket back into his crate.

'There you go again, bro,' said Mali. 'Acting like the big old dragon. What makes you so important, eh?'

'I'll tell you exactly what, ar' kid,' he snarled. 'Because I've just received word from Vainclaw. We have a new assignment.'

Flotsam's ears pricked up. 'No more cats?' he asked hopefully.

'Yeah, spill the beans, like. What's the job?' asked Jegsy.

'Stage two,' said Leon.

'Oh yeah,' said his brother. 'Then why didn't he tell the rest of us?'

'Because Vainclaw trusts me,' Leon said pointedly.

'Bully for you,' Mali sulked.

'Forget your usual routes. Today, you're all to follow me.'

'Where are we going?' asked Flotsam.

'I told you. It's time for stage two,' replied Leon.

'I don't believe you,' said Mali. 'The big V man ain't told you nothing.'

'Yes, he has,' said Leon impatiently .

'Has not.'

'Has so.'

'Cut it out,' said Flotsam. 'I think we should just . . . ah . . . ah . . . ah . . .'

The other three dragons cowered in anticipation.

'Ah . . . ah . . .'

After a moment's pause, Flotsam sniffed and said, 'Actually, I think I'm all right.'

He wiped his nose, and the other dragons raised their heads, looking relieved.

'CHOOOOO!' he screamed, fire bursting from his

mouth.

'I could give you something for that,' said Jegsy, diving once again into the crate. 'Take one of these every hour until the sneezing stops,' he said, passing Flotsam a selection of tennis balls.

'Thanks,' said the Sea Dragon, putting one into his mouth and biting down. 'It's a bit chewy,' he said.

'Maybe it should be dissolved in water first,' said the other.

'Can you stop messing around?' barked Leon. 'Come on, everyone follow me.'

Dirk kept very still.

The large, yellow-backed Scavenger flew up to the skylight.

Dirk held his breath.

The dragon slid the skylight open, slipped through the hole and disappeared on to the roof. The other three dragons followed. As the last one slid the skylight shut, Dirk heard the one called Leon say, 'Remember, no robbing, no arguing and no sneezing.'

Once he was sure that they had gone Dirk flew to the skylight, his skin returning to its true colour. He slid it open and slipped out on to the roof. He could see the four dragons leaping from roof to roof, the large, yellow one leading the way. He was about to take chase when he noticed out of the corner of his eye a light-blue, round-topped car, parked by the side of the warehouse. Inside the car Dirk could see Mrs Klingerflim sitting, smiling vaguely and tapping her hands on the steering wheel. *Holly*, he thought. *Why isn't Holly with her?*

Checking no one was around, he jumped down to the street below and approached the car window, where Mrs Klingerflim was listening to some old crackly music on the radio. It sounded like an awful noise to Dirk, but she seemed to be enjoying it.

'Mrs Klingerflim,' he said.

'Is that you, Mr Dilly?' she said, turning to look at him. 'You made me jump. What are you doing here?'

'Where's Holly?'

'I don't know, dear,' replied the old lady. 'She said she would only be a minute.'

'Rats,' said Dirk. He looked around. The once-white van was gone. He flew back to the roof, but still couldn't see any sign of it. He needed height and he needed it now. Three roofs away was a large industrial chimney. He ran across the roof, dived to the next, landing into a forward roll, and then he was springing up, spreading his wings and flying to the top of the chimney. Carefully balancing on the rim he looked down at the surrounding streets. There was still no sign of the van. And then he saw another car he recognised. It was the grey Mercedes with the white stripe that had been parked outside his flat, the one driven by the man in the wide-brimmed hat. It was driving full pelt away, jumping every red light it went through, heading eastward.

Dirk spread his wings, and leapt from the chimney, taking chase as the sun set behind him.

Chapter Eighteen

The car took the same route out of the city that the two crooks had taken in the van. It parked in front of the church, across the road from the shady path that led to the riverside. Dirk landed on the church roof. The man in the wide-brimmed hat got out and hurried across the road. He walked briskly down the path, his hands thrust deep in his pockets, his head bowed down. He was alone.

Cursing himself for not having his disguise with him, Dirk swooped down to the car. There was no sign of Holly in the front seat. No sign in the back. Ears pricked up, listening for anyone approaching, Dirk slipped round the back of the car. He lowered his head to the boot and said, 'Holly, are you in there?'

Nothing.

He opened his mouth and clamped his teeth down on the boot, being careful not to bite straight through the metal. The last thing he wanted was to skewer the girl on one of his teeth. Satisfied with his grip he raised his head slowly. It made an awful sound, of teeth against steel. *There goes my enamel,* thought Dirk. He pushed the door wide open, braced himself and looked down. She wasn't there.

'Rancid rats called Rodney,' Dirk swore, jumping back to the safety of the church roof just as a solitary furniture removal van rumbled past. It was late and with only a few yellow street lamps to combat the darkness, Dirk could barely make out the man in the wide-brimmed hat. In a matter of seconds he would disappear from sight altogether, into the shadows.

The road was clear. Dirk spread his wings, stood on tiptoes on the edge of the church, his forepaws stretched out like an Olympic diver, made a tiny jump and glided across the road, down the path, gathering speed as he flew.

Dirk cut silently through the air towards the man.

He knew he had one chance to get this right.

Centimetres away from the man's back, Dirk swung his feet down, clamped the man's shoulder with his right forepaw and thrust his index claw into the small of his back, as though it were a gun.

The man froze, then raised his arms. 'I'm not armed,' he said.

'Don't turn around,' Dirk whispered in his ear. 'I'll shoot if I have to. Now start talking.'

'What d'you want to talk about?' replied the man casually.

'Your favourite brand of baked beans,' said Dirk. 'What do you think?'

'I prefer spaghetti hoops and you're going to have to be more specific,' he retorted.

He was talking coolly. Dirk could tell that this wasn't the first time that the man had felt a gun pushed against his back. It was, however, probably the first time that the gun had actually been a very sharp claw belonging to a red-backed, green-bellied, urban-based Mountain Dragon.

'OK. Let's start with your name,' said Dirk.

'Blake,' said the man. 'Ladbroke Blake.'

'Ladbroke Blake,' he said. 'Sort of name that would look good on a gravestone.'

'Is that supposed to be a threat?'

'Just answer my questions, buddy. It's been a long day.'

'Give me a question I can answer then, buddy,' replied Ladbroke.

'Where's the girl?'

'I could ask you the same thing.'

'Except that I'm the one holding the gun.' Dirk pushed his claw further into the man's back.

'All right, take it easy. I haven't touched her. I was just hired to follow her. OK?'

'Who hired you?' asked Dirk.

'There is such a thing as client confidentiality,' said Ladbroke.

'Honour amongst thieves, eh?' smirked the dragon.

'I'm not a thief. I'm a private detective. My card is in my top pocket.'

'OK,' said Dirk. 'Carefully, without making any sudden movements and using your left hand, pull it out and show it to me.'

Ladbroke pulled out a business card and held it up.

'Dr Hilary Fletch,' read Dirk. 'Forensic specialist and part-time pathologist?'

'Oh, sorry,' said Ladbroke. 'Wrong card. Try this one.'

He pulled out another. It read:

LADBROKE BLAKE

BLAKE INVESTIGATIONS:

Confidential, Professional and
Affordable Private Investigations

'Nice card,' said Dirk.

'Thanks. I just got new ones from the printer. Romalian typeface on Eggshell, whatever that means.'

'I'm not interested in your typeface, Blake. Just tell me who hired you or I'll be asking you to investigate the bottom of the Thames.'

'That's another threat, isn't it?'

'Who?' demanded Dirk, tightening his grip on the man's shoulder.

'Mrs Bigsby, Holly's mother.'

'You mean her dad's wife,' replied Dirk.

'Well, it's a good job she did hire me. This isn't your average truant case. It seems that young Holly has got herself mixed up in some serious trouble.'

'What do you know?' asked Dirk anxiously.

'I know that she's been hanging around with some crazy, blind, old lady, who drives like a lunatic. I know that the old lady gave her a lift to a warehouse in East London this evening, where she was forced into the back of a dirty white van – license plate K884 UTA – at gunpoint by two low-life thugs and that they drove her here and that right now she's about fifty metres in that direction.' Dirk could tell he was telling the truth. 'Now will you let me go?'

'No problem,' said Dirk. He released the detective from his grip, but before he could turn round, whacked him over the head. Ladbroke Blake fell to the ground in a slump. Dirk checked his pulse. He was fine, just unconscious. He dragged the body under a hedge and continued carefully down the path, wondering what sort of stepmother hires a private detective because her daughter is bunking off school.

His thoughts were interrupted by approaching voices. Dirk dived behind a tree.

'Hey, Arthur, what was that?' said the first voice.

'Don't be so paranoid, Reg. It was probably just a fox,' said the second.

'This job just gets worse and worse. First cats, now little girls. It's not right. It's not normal.'

'Imagine, Reg, that you are in a room. Can you imagine that?'

'What sort of room?' asked Reg.

The two crooks passed where Dirk was hiding.

'A very boring room, Reg, one with just a chair in it and a picture of some flowers in a bowl. Imagine you are in a boring room like that and then you leave.'

'Because it's so boring?'

'Yes, Reg. The question is, once you have left, how do you know the room still exists?'

'Because I've just been there.'

The voices grew fainter as the men got further away.

'But you are no longer there. You have left. How do you know it still exists?

'I don't think I follow you,' said Reg.

'Forget the girl. She no longer exists. Think about the money,' replied Arthur.

The two men gone, Dirk continued down the path, which opened on to the clearing by the river, where he saw the once-white van parked. He made three steps towards it then stopped. His ears pricked up. He could hear the whirring of approaching dragon wings. He dived for cover just as the four Kinghorn dragons landed by the side of the van.

Heads lowered, they prowled silently towards the

vehicle, glancing from side to side as they moved. The Mountain Dragon and the Sea Dragon stopped on either side of the van. The small Scavenger hopped on top. The large one, Leon, walked to the back, raised himself up on his hind legs, grabbed the handles, and pulled the door open. The sound of a young girl screaming filled the air.

Holly, thought Dirk.

'Ar-right, calm down,' he heard the large Scavenger say, jumping into the van. '*I'm* not going to hurt you.'

The Sea Dragon and the Mountain Dragon snig-gered, rounded the van and, using their tails, slammed the doors shut.

The screaming stopped.

Chapter Nineteen

Dirk watched the three dragons guarding the van. He had to help Holly but even he couldn't take on all three of them. Not all at once, anyway. As quietly as possible he backed into the undergrowth then headed down the path.

In the back of the once-white van, the dragon's large ugly face loomed close to Holly's. A droplet of spittle fell from one of its long, sharp teeth on to her jeans. It sniffed Holly's hair, and brought its enormous yellow eyes to peer at her face. Dirk had been right. Its breath stank. Holly moved her head away as much as she could, but the two crooks had tied the ropes too tightly. The dragon examined her up and down.

'Scared, are you?' it asked.

'I'm not scared of you,' she replied defiantly. 'You're just a coward.'

'Coward, eh? We'll see how brave you are in a minute.'

'Well, carry on, if it makes you feel big to pick on girls and defenceless cats.'

'What do you know about the cats?' snapped the dragon.

'I know you've been stealing them. I know about the Kinghorns. And I know about Vainclaw Grandin.'

For a moment, Holly thought she saw fear in the dragon's yellow eyes. It pushed its face up to hers. The breath was unbearable, like it had been gargling with toilet water. 'Where did you hear that name?' it demanded.

'Why are you doing this?' she asked.

'This is war. How do you know about . . .' the dragon lowered his voice to a whisper, 'Vainclaw?'

'But we're not at war. Anyway, what does it matter what I know. You're going to kill me, anyway, aren't you?'

'True. And not just you. Soon your whole pathetic race will be extinct.'

'But why?' she asked.

'Because we hate you, all of you. Humans have always been terrified of the big scaly creature lurking beneath the surface, waiting to rear its ugly head and feast on the fair maiden, always relying on the knight in shining armour to turn up at the last minute to kill the creature, save the maiden and take all the glory. Well, have you ever thought about this? Maybe the maiden never needed saving. Maybe the creature doesn't need killing. Maybe it's the knight that's the problem.'

Outside the van the Sea Dragon, Flotsam, was getting jittery. 'What was that noise?' he said, glancing fearfully at the trees.

'What noise?' asked Jegsy. 'I didn't hear no noise.'

'Over there. I heard something.'

'What you two talking about?' spat Mali, circling the top of the van.

'Flotsam's hearing noises, like,' said Jegsy.

'Well, go and check it out, then,' said Mali.

'On my own? What if it's a . . . a human?' stammered Flotsam, looking scared.

'Flotsam, you idiot! You're a dragon,' said Mali, 'You have razor-sharp talons, teeth that could snap a man in half, an armour-plated back and you can breathe fire. What are you scared of?'

'But it's still breaching the forbidden divide,' Flotsam shuddered. 'We're not supposed to be seen.'

'You fool,' spat Mali. 'What's it matter if anyone sees you at this stage?'

'That's true, like,' said Jegsy. 'It don't matter.'

'Still, can't one of you come with me?' pleaded Flotsam.

'I'll come,' said Jegsy. 'I don't mind.'

'Go on, then, hurry up,' said Mali. 'Remember the plan.'

The two dragons walked into the overgrown wooded area cautiously. With each step it got darker and they grew closer together, until they were walking shoulder to shoulder.

'Look, someone's there,' whispered Flotsam.

Jegsy looked. Sure enough he could make out a figure. It looked like a man, wearing a long raincoat and a wide-brimmed hat.

'Come on,' said Jegsy.

'What if he's armed?' asked Flotsam. 'They have guns, remember.'

'I'll go round the back, surround him, like,' said Jegsy. 'We'll do the old surround-and-pounce plan.'

'What's the old surround-and-pounce plan?' asked

Flotsam.

'Well, we surround him, then we pounce on him.'

'Oh yeah,' said Flotsam, and Jegsy disappeared into the darkness, leaving Flotsam to creep slowly towards the unmoving shadowy figure, stepping as lightly as possible. Once he was near enough he crouched down. Jegsy moved into position on the other side of the man. Then, in one sudden movement, they both leapt forward, landing on top of him. But instead of feeling a solid body crumbling beneath them, they heard a stick snap and both fell heavily to the ground. They looked at each other in confusion.

'There's no one here, like,' said Jegsy.

'Why would someone leave their clothes here?' replied Flotsam.

'Dunno,' said Jegsy, shrugging. 'Neat hat though,' he said, picking up the wide-brimmed hat, examining it then placing it on his head. 'Hey, I think it suits me? What do you think, Flotsam? Flotsam?'

Jegsy turned to look at the other dragon. Flotsam was lying flat out on the ground.

That's why the clothes were there, thought Jegsy. It was a trap. His suspicion was confirmed when he felt a sharp pain on the back of his head and he was knocked out.

Clinging to the thick trunk of the oak above the two unconscious dragons, Dirk Dilly swung his trusty tail back up and smiled. Then he dropped to the ground, and headed towards the riverfront.

'Two down,' he muttered.

For a moment Holly thought the dragon was going to bite her. She closed her eyes, but his teeth fell just short, cutting through the ropes that were holding her down.

'Out,' said the Scavenger, backing out and knocking the doors wide open. Holly followed him out. 'And no funny business. Unless you want to be toast.'

Stepping out of the van Holly could see the other yellow-backed dragon on the roof. It stared at her intently.

'Where are the others, ar' kid?' asked the larger brother.

'They went to check out a noise that Flotsam heard,' said Mali.

'Idiots. Come on, let's get the girl in place.'

The other dragon jumped down and nudged Holly towards the river. 'Move,' he said.

Her heart beating fast, she walked to where the wooden raft was once again drawn in. 'Get on,' said the smaller dragon.

'What are you going to do to me?' she asked.

'*I'm* not going to do anything to you. Get on,' said the dragon, shoving her with his nose so that she slipped down the bank and on to the raft, which wobbled unstably. She dropped to her knees and clung to the base to avoid falling in, but water lapped over the top, soaking her jeans, and making her hands bitterly cold.

Without another word, the dragon let the rope out and nudged the raft just as Holly had seen the two crooks do before. Caught by the current, the raft bobbed out on to the dark river. The two yellow dragons watched from the shore, getting further and further away. Holly was alone, like she had never been in her life. And scared. For the first time in a long, long time she felt a genuine tear fall down her cheek.

Quietly, in the middle of the cold river, with no one to hear, she wept.

Chapter Twenty

Dirk watched Holly drifting out on to the river. Poor kid. She looked terrified. He needed to work fast, but he also needed to work smart and that was tricky when he hadn't got the faintest idea what was going on. Not even an inkling. There was something out there and it was dangerous. But what? If he flew over and grabbed Holly the two yellows would see him and he would only endanger her even more. No, he needed a plan.

A twig snapped. He froze. Someone was behind him, creeping up on him. Dirk waited for his moment, acting like he hadn't heard anything, then suddenly he lashed his tail across the ground, knocking his assailant's feet from under him. He spun round, his claws drawn.

Lying on the ground was a dragon. Dirk stepped forward, but it lashed out its tail, catching his feet, knocking him on to his belly. Before he could get up, he felt the dragon land on his back, pinning him down, but its grip wasn't good enough. Dirk spun round, sending his attacker flying. He sprang to his feet, whacked the dragon's head with his tail, jumped up and kicked him hard in the belly, knocking him backwards.

'Dirk, it's me. Don't hurt me,' whined the dragon. 'It's Karnataka,'

'Karny?' said Dirk, taken aback. 'What are you doing here? You're above ground.'

'Don't I know it? It's a lot darker than it used to be, up here. I like it. What happened?'

'It's night-time, Karny.'

'Oh right. That explains it,' said Karnataka. 'Do you mind?'

'Oh, sorry.' Dirk backed off, allowing the Shade-Hugger to get up. 'How did you know I was here?' asked Dirk.

'I didn't,' Karnataka replied. 'I wanted to see if it was true for myself, what they've got in there.'

'You know what it is?' said Dirk.

Karnataka nodded.

'Spill the beans, Karny.'

'Spill the liquorice, Dilly,' said Karnataka.

'I'll get it later.' Dirk wasn't in the mood for games.

'No liquorice, no info. That's the rule.'

'Karny, tell me what they've got before I toast your tail,' Dirk said threateningly.

'All right, because it's you but I expect double next time I see you. And laces, make sure you bring laces.'

'Tell me,' growled Dirk.

Karnataka lowered his voice. 'They've got an Amphiptere in there,' he whispered.

'How big?' asked Dirk.

'It's a female,' replied Karnataka, eyes wide with fear. 'A big one.'

Amphipteres were ancient beasts, older even than dragons. Dirk hadn't met many of them as they tended to avoid all contact with both humans and dragons, hiding in the deepest regions of the oceans. Dirk recalled one he had encountered while on a case in Egypt. It was twice the size of him, with a snake-like body, two large wings and a long, flowing mane. But as soon as it saw him it had disappeared. Amphipteres were not social creatures. And they grew big. The females grew really big.

'So, that's what knocked me out?' said Dirk.

'You must have swallowed some of its blood when you bit into it,' replied Karnataka. 'You're lucky you're still around at all.'

'But what's it doing here?' asked Dirk.

'The word is that they're holding it here with a chain made from black metal, the stuff the Dragnet use. Not even an Amphiptere can bite through that stuff,' replied Karnataka.

'It doesn't make sense,' said Dirk. 'Amphipteres are vegetarians like us. Why would they be feeding it cats?'

Their conversation was cut short by a flash of fire. Dirk jumped to avoid it but felt something land on top of him. A large, yellow face appeared in front of his. Its mouth opened and a flame burst forth. The fire ceased and the dragon's face reappeared. Before Dirk could retaliate he felt a sharp claw under his chin, preventing his mouth from opening.

The large Scavenger yelled, 'I got me a Mountain Dragon here. What you got, Mali?'

Out of the corner of his eye Dirk could see Karnataka also lying on his back with the smaller of the two yellow-backs on his belly.

'Shade-Hugger, by the looks of things, Leon.'

'Above ground? Must be lost,' he said. 'Now start talking, mountain boy.'

'We're researching a new, fresh-breath, minty mouthwash for dragons,' murmured Dirk through his teeth. 'You should try it.'

'Eh, this one's got a sense of humour, Mali.'

'I'm not joking. You have some kind of problem,' said Dirk.

'Can we kill 'em, bro?' said Mali.

'Not yet, ar' kid. Humans is one things, but we can't have the Council finding out about all this. Remember, it's supposed to look like an accident.' He turned to Dirk. 'What's your name? And what do you know?'

'I'm the Loch Ness monster and I know that your breath smells like you've been snacking on badger droppings,' replied Dirk.

The dragon jammed its claw further into his jaw, drawing dark-green blood that trickled down his chin.

'What about you?' Mali asked Karnataka.

'My name's Karnataka,' he said quickly, 'I'm only here because he asked me to find out what you were doing?'

'Nice,' said Dirk. 'Thanks, Karny. I knew I could rely on you.'

'Why?' asked Mali.

'He's a private detective,' said the dragon, shaking with fear. 'He works in the human world.'

'And did you find out what we're doing?'

Karnataka nodded.

'Eh, what's going on, like?' said another voice.

The Mountain Dragon and the Sea Dragon appeared, rubbing their heads.

'Where have you been?' demanded Leon.

'They attacked us,' said Flotsam.

'It wasn't me,' said Karnataka. 'It was just him.'

'Again, cheers,' said Dirk.

'Move!' ordered Leon. 'The show is about to start. And you two have just earned yourselves front-row tickets.' He turned to address Jegsy and Flotsam. 'Come on, you idiots, make yourselves useful,' he said.

The two dragons stood over Dirk and Karnataka as the brothers released them.

'One step out of line and you're charcoal, OK, Mr Detective?' said Leon, releasing Dirk.

The four dragons surrounded Dirk and Karnataka and led them out of the trees into the clearing by the river, emitting bursts of fire to keep them in line. The odds weren't good. Even if Karnataka fought on his side, Dirk and he were outnumbered two to one. And those were exactly the kind of odds that would make a dragon like Karnataka think twice about fighting on his side.

They stopped by the wooden post that kept the raft in place and Leon opened his mouth and burnt straight through the rope, setting the raft adrift.

He picked up the remaining rope in his teeth and, with the others' help, pushed Dirk and Karnataka into place and tied them back to back against the post.

Wrapping the ropes round Dirk's mouth, Leon said, 'Don't want you burning your way out, do we?'

He pulled a large, dark, metal key shaped like a dragon's head from behind his wing and threw it at Flotsam. 'It's time to give her some slack,' he said. 'Make sure she can't escape, mind.'

Flotsam caught the key and dived into the river.

They waited in silence for a couple of minutes and then the water began to lap against the shore as though a boat had just passed. But there was no sign of a boat.

Flotsam climbed out of the river and said, 'She's coming up.'

* * *

Holly lay flat on the raft, which rocked violently from side to side. Her hands were numb with cold; her clothes, soaking wet. Her body shivered and her teeth chattered. She had gone beyond crying. She was too scared to feel any self-pity. All that was left now was fear. Desperately she grabbed the rope, but it came too easily. It had been cut loose. The undercurrent was too strong to swim. She was stranded.

Something broke the surface. It was as though a grassy island was slowly emerging from under the water. A light appeared in the side of it, round like a full moon, but fire-red and bigger than Holly's head. She was trying to work out what it was when another one appeared. They blinked. They were eyes. This was no island. It was an enormous head. What she had seen as long strands of grass was, in fact, a thick mane of hair.

It opened its mouth, revealing hundreds of teeth, and then suddenly the head shot high into the sky, followed by its long body, like a giant oak tree shooting from the water. The creature unfurled two expansive wings. And all the time more and more of its smooth serpentine body appeared from the depths below.

Even fear left Holly now. There was no escape. No hope. She was going to die. She clung to the raft and awaited her fate.

Chapter Twenty-One

Dirk watched the Amphiptere appear. He had never seen one this big, nor this far inland. It flapped its wings and roared. He could imagine the panic on the faces of the humans in the surrounding area that could see it, but there was only one human he was worried about. Holly.

'We call her Mandy,' said the large Scavenger, laughing. 'Hey, ar' kid, keep an eye on Mr Detective here.'

'Keep an eye on him yourself,' replied Mali.

'When are you going to understand that I'm in charge?' asked Leon.

'When your name is Vainclaw, that's when. He's the boss.'

'But while he's not here, I am.'

'Oh yeah?' challenged Mali.

The two dragons squared up to each other.

'Eh, you two, leave it out,' said Flotsam. 'Shouldn't we get going?'

'I want to see if she eats the human,' replied Leon.

Having reached her full height, three times higher than any surrounding buildings, the Amphiptere was flailing in the water, making an awful screeching noise.

Dirk needed a plan. His legs were bound tightly and his mouth was tied shut but his tail was free. He stretched it as far as he could. The dragons were all just out of reach.

'Flotsam's right. We should get going,' said Mali.

'Ar-right, blueberry boy, we'll go in a minute,' said Leon.

'Don't call me that,' snarled his brother.

'Give it a rest, like,' said Jegsy.

'Take it back,' said Mali.

'Ar-right, ar kid. Calm down, I take it back,' said Leon, taking a couple of steps back, bringing him just in reach. Dirk stretched out his tail, aimed carefully, then whacked Leon's backside with the tip, before quickly drawing it back to his side.

'What d'you do that for?' Leon said to Mali.

'Do what?'

'Oh, don't come the innocent with me, if you want a fight, just say so.'

'I'm ready any time, bro. You want a piece of me?'

The dragons stood nose to nose. Smoke billowed from their nostrils then Leon reared up on to his hind legs and sent a burst of fire from his mouth. Mali ducked and it missed him, instead singeing Dirk's chest. It hurt like hell, but it had done the job. It had burnt straight through the rope. Dirk hastily grabbed the charred ends and held them together, but the dragons were too preoccupied to notice, Jegsy and Flotsam holding the brothers away from each other.

'Come on, lads, there's no need for this,' said Jesgy.

'Yeah, we haven't got time,' said Flotsam. 'We should go.'

'We go when I say so,' said Leon, turning on the Sea Dragon.

'But what about Mandy?' asked Flotsam, pointing at the Amphiptere thrashing around in the water.

'Yeah, what about her, like?' said Jegsy.

'It's true, bro,' agreed Mali. 'We hang around much longer and there won't be anything much left of us to fight.'

'I have decided,' announced Leon, 'that we should go.'

The other three dragons looked visibly relieved. Leon turned to Dirk, who bowed his head to hide the loose rope.

'Enjoy the show, Mr Detective,' he said. 'See you round, Shade-Hugger,' he added to Karnataka.

'Mwhmnmmrmdl,' replied Karnataka, wriggling to get free.

Dirk was glad Karnataka's mouth was still bound. No one likes to hear a grown dragon beg for mercy.

Leon slapped his tail hard against Dirk's face and said, 'That's for sticking your big, green, mountain nose into other dragons' business.' He turned to the others and said, 'Let's go.'

All four spread their wings and took to the sky, flying into the night without another glance back.

The Kinghorns had gone.

Dirk shook the ropes off and released Karnataka from the ropes and said, 'I need your help, Karny. Holly's in danger. I need you to grab her while I distract the Amphiptere, OK?'

'Of course, Dirk,' said Karnataka, standing up. 'You can rely on me, Dirk. When have I ever let you down, Dirk?'

'Right, come on, then,' said Dirk, spreading his

wings and rising into the air.

'Just one thing, Dirk,' said Karnataka.

'What?'

'I know what they've got planned for Mandy and if you take my advice you'll forget the human and get out of here now,' he replied, turning, dropping down on to all fours and running full pelt into the trees.

'Rats in white satin!' swore Dirk.

He could have caught him of course, but what was the point? He couldn't force him to help. It would just be a waste of time and if there was one thing he didn't have a lot of, it was time.

'Should have seen that coming really,' he muttered, flying towards the Amphiptere.

Holly looked up at the creature. It flapped its wings, lifting its huge head high in the sky, and pulling its body straight. It was enormous. Having reached a great height it began to swoop down, its drooling cavernous mouth heading straight for her. Dirk had said that there were bigger, scarier things in the world than dragons, but never in her wildest nightmares had she imagined anything this big or this scary.

She screamed and clung to the rocking raft. The head grew nearer. She could see right down its throat. Its mouth began to close and she felt certain that this would be the last thing she ever saw. She closed her eyes, hoping only that she would die quickly and painlessly.

The mouth crashed shut and Holly felt strangely weightless. She could no longer feel the damp wood under her knees or the cold water lapping over her fingers.

She opened her eyes and saw the raft. Only now it was a metre below her, bobbing up and down on the waves.

Slowly she craned her neck round and found herself looking into two enormous, red eyes. The hideous creature had caught her belt in its teeth and was holding her in the air. For a moment they stared unblinkingly into each other's eyes.

Then the creature turned its head, causing Holly to lurch to one side. Something had distracted it. She turned to see what and saw through the darkness a bright-orange flame speeding towards them, reflecting on the water's surface, growing bigger and brighter as it got nearer.

The creature opened its mouth and reared its head. Holly fell back on to the raft, which rocked violently. She lost her footing and slipped into the icy river.

Sound cut out. She floated down through the murky water, numbed by the cold, feeling peaceful. Tranquil. Then something grabbed her and heaved her, spluttering and coughing, back on to the raft. She gasped for breath and looked up.

'Come on,' said the familiar voice of Dirk Dilly. 'I don't think this structure is very stable.'

Looking up at him, the relief she felt instantly seeped away as, behind him, the creature's head was hurtling towards them at great speed.

'Jump on,' said Dirk, helping her on to his back. 'Hold on tight.'

The head was almost upon them.

'Go!' screamed Holly.

Dirk leapt off the raft and flew into the air. Holly looked behind her and saw the creature grab hold of the raft and crush it between its teeth, splinters flying everywhere.

Her body was soaking wet. She ached all over and tears of fear and relief were streaming down her face. The only words she could manage were, 'I thought I was going to die.'

'Never,' said Dirk. 'I wouldn't let anything happen to my partner.'

Chapter Twenty-Two

Dirk touched down on the riverbank by the van and Holly climbed off his back, grateful to feel solid ground beneath her feet. The Amphiptere howled and thrashed wildly in the water.

'What's it doing?' asked Holly.

'They've chained her to the river bed,' said Dirk. 'She's trapped.'

'She could have eaten me, but she didn't.'

'Eating meat would have the same effect on her as it would on me.'

'Why? What is it?' she asked.

'An Amphiptere. Limbless dragons from an ancient time before dinosaurs,' said Dirk. 'She's called Mandy.'

'Well, Mandy's attracting a lot of attention,' said Holly.

Lights had come on in the flats and houses all around. People were standing at the windows, staring in horror or gesticulating at the monstrous creature hissing and snarling in the water. The sound of panic filled the air and Holly could hear approaching sirens.

'The police,' she said.

'Racing rats from Rickmansworth!' exclaimed Dirk, slapping himself hard in the face. 'That's it. That's what they're up to. We've got to save her.'

'Save her?' asked Holly. 'From what?'

'Mandy may look scary,' explained Dirk, 'but her skin is as thin as paper. Her main defence against attack is her poisonous blood. Look what happened when I bit into her. I was unconscious for three days and I'm a healthy young dragon. But poisonous blood is no defence against bullets.' Dirk picked up the rope that had held him captive and tied one end of it round his waist.

'So what about the cats?' asked Holly.

'Fresh meat. They've been forcing her to eat the cats.'

'But that will kill her,' she said.

'Yes, but first her blood will boil and more importantly turn to gas.' He tied the other end of the rope to the post and checked the length. 'Then they put you out as bait and unleash the monster, so when the police arrive they find Mandy apparently attacking you. They open fire and BOOM.'

'The knights in shining armour slay the monster.'

'Yes. They put more holes into Mandy than it would take to fill the Albert Hall, releasing enough poisonous gas into the atmosphere to wipe out every living creature in a ten-mile radius.'

'So Mandy's a bomb?'

'Exactly,' said Dirk. 'And the boys in blue here are loaded up with the detonators.'

White headlights were shining through the trees. Cars were driving down the path to the clearing.

'Can you bite through the chains?' said Holly.

'No, it's black metal forged in the fire of the Outer Core. It's twenty times stronger than any human metal,' said Dirk. 'I'll have to bite through the thinnest part of Mandy I can find.'

'But won't that release the gas?'

'Some, yes, but Amphiptere skin grows back pretty quickly near the tail. It'll be enough to knock me out, but this rope should make sure I can find my way back. Try to stop them shooting at it,' said Dirk, diving head first into the water with a splash just as a headlight swung across the darkness, illuminating Holly.

She watched the coiled rope unravel as Dirk pulled on the other end.

A car screeched to a halt. She turned round, squinting into the lights. More appeared. Police cars and vans stopped in front of her. Blinded by the brightness, Holly heard car doors open, crackling police radios, people shouting orders, a spotlight coming on and shining up at the Amphiptere and the sound of guns being cocked.

'No!' yelled Holly. 'Don't shoot. Don't shoot.'

A silhouetted figure emerged from the bright lights. 'Hold your fire,' he said, walking forward. As he got nearer, Holly could make out the policeman's bearded face, his eyes staring up in bewilderment at the huge creature in front of him.

'What . . . is . . . it?' he said quietly.

'Don't let them shoot,' Holly pleaded.

'What is it?' he asked again, his gaze fixed firmly on the beast.

'It's an Amphiptere,' said Holly. 'Her blood is poisonous and it's turned to gas because she's been eating meat, and if you shoot her you'll release it and wipe out the entire city.'

The policeman looked down at Holly, then back up again. 'What is it?' he said.

A second policeman joined them and said, 'Do you want us to open fire, sir? Sir? Detective Inspector Hughes, sir? Are you all right, sir?' he said.

'Sergeant?' said the stunned policeman.

'Yes, sir.'

'What is it?'

'I would describe it as a huge winged serpent of the variety that hitherto was only thought to have existed in the mythological writings of the ancient Egyptians and such like,' said the sergeant.

'It's a bomb,' said Holly. 'Don't shoot it.'

'A bomb?' said the sergeant. 'No, bombs are a lot smaller than that and rarely have wings or heads. That's your basic winged serpent, that is. Should we shoot it, sir?'

The bearded policeman looked at him, blinked and said, 'What? Yes, shoot it. Shoot it down.'

'No,' said Holly. 'You'll kill us all.'

'Sorry, miss, we're just following protocol,' said the sergeant. 'Anything seen by officers of the law that does not conform to the conventional understanding of the world as we know it is to be shot on sight.'

'But it's not attacking. Look.'

'Just because it's not attacking, doesn't mean it's not going to attack,' he said, grabbing her arm and dragging her behind the cars, followed by the dazed detective inspector. Struggling to get free Holly saw a line of guns raised up, aiming at the Amphiptere's head.

'No!' she cried. 'Don't.'

'Shall we fire now, sir?'

'What?' said the detective inspector, still transfixed. 'Yes, fire. Shoot. Kill it.'

'Ready,' shouted the sergeant at the top of his voice. 'Aim for the head, lads . . . And fire!'

Holly shielded her ears as an explosion of bullets took to the air, sounding like thunder.

Dirk swam through the murky water, fighting against the strong undercurrent. *I'm swimming in the Mediterranean*, he thought. *It's a lovely sunny day and I've gone for a swim to cool off. It certainly isn't the River Thames and I am certainly not about to bite into something that will poison me and possibly kill me. Oh no, I'm on holiday.*

There were lights swirling over the river's surface

and Dirk could make out the end of the Amphiptere's long body, snaking down through the water. He tried to swim towards it but felt a tug on his belly. The rope wasn't long enough. He had no choice. He untied it and let it go. It floated away into the darkness. He would have to find his own way back.

Dirk followed the tail down to the bottom of the river, where it was at its thinnest. He stood on the river bed and looked up. It looked as if the body went on for ever, but Dirk knew that somewhere up there it did have an end and at that end was the head of a scared, long-maned, female Amphiptere called Mandy, with the potential to wipe out every living creature in London.

Here goes, he thought, grabbing the tail to hold it still. He opened his mouth, letting in the foul river water.

I'm on holiday, he thought, *I'm in the Med enjoying a lovely bit of celery. Mmm, celery*. He bit down. His teeth sliced through the tail, splitting it in clean in two. He felt the rancid taste on his tongue and the water darkened.

Lethargy washed over him.

His eyelids grew heavy.

His body felt weak.

Bubbles, he thought, *there are no bubbles*.

Then he blacked out.

Chapter Twenty-Three

The gunfire stopped but the noise reverberated around Holly's ears. A cloud of smoke wafted in front of them. *This is it*, she thought. They had failed. The bullets had penetrated the skin and the poison was spreading through the atmosphere. The Kinghorns had won.

She waited.

But nothing happened.

The smoke from the gunfire cleared to reveal the empty river in front of them, calm again.

'Did we hit it?' asked the detective inspector.

'Spotlight,' shouted the sergeant and a spotlight on the back of a van swung its beam across the surface of the water. There was no sign of the Amphiptere.

'Should we send in the divers, sir?'

'What? Yes, good idea. Send in the divers.'

'Get the divers!' shouted the sergeant.

'You must have missed it,' said Holly.

'That's very unlikely,' said the sergeant. 'We have some excellent marksmen in the force. Wilkins over there won a prize last year, didn't you, Wilkins?'

Another policeman gave a little wave and shouted proudly, 'Best shot in Barking three years in a row, sir.'

'But we'd all be dead if you'd hit it,' she said.

'You seem to know a lot about this,' said the bearded policeman, who had snapped out of his trance. 'My name is Detective Inspector Hughes. And what, may I ask, is your name?' he demanded.

'Holly.'

'And how do you profess to know so much, Holly?'

'I . . .' Holly stopped herself from bursting out with everything she knew. The Kinghorns. The cats. The plan to blow up London. Dirk had said that if humans knew dragons existed then there would be a war.

'Are you alone?' asked Detective Inspector Hughes.

'Yes,' said Holly.

She glanced at the rope which led into the river then quickly looked away, but the policeman followed her gaze and asked, 'What's on the end of this, then?'

'Nothing,' she replied. 'I don't know.'

'Sergeant, haul in that rope,' ordered Hughes.

The sergeant grabbed it and pulled it in easily. Dirk was no longer tied to the other end. Holly's relief that they hadn't found him was measured by thoughts of what might have happened to him.

'OK, little girl,' said the detective inspector, 'start talking,'

Holly opened her mouth to speak, but before she could utter one word her attention was drawn by the sound of a slow handclap. She and both policemen turned to see a man in a long coat and a wide-brimmed hat walking slowly towards them, clapping his hands together.

'*Bravo! Bravissimo!* Well done. Tallulah you are an a-genius. Even when the camera is not a-pointing at you, you continue.' The man spoke in an Italian accent, gesticulating flamboyantly. 'This is real method acting. You make De Niro look like an am dram theatre ham. I will call him tomorrow and tell him as much.'

'Who are you?' barked Detective Inspector Hughes.

'My name is Alfonso Firenze. I am a great film director. This is my card.' The man pulled out a card from his top pocket and the sergeant took it.

'Alfonzo Firenze,' he read aloud, 'director, producer, writer and genius.'

'Oh, ha ha, a little joke.' The man laughed again. 'I never write.'

'And you know this girl?' said Detective Inspector Hughes.

'Is it a-possible that you do *not* know this girl?' demanded the man. 'Look at her. Do you not a-recognise her? She is Tallulah Manderville, the greatest child actor of our time. You should see her cry. It is a-beautiful. Cry for the policeman, Tallulah. Cry.'

'Er . . .' Holly was unsure how to react. She recognised him as the man who had been following Dirk. She had no idea who he was, but something in his kind, well-worn face made her want to trust him.

'Cry. Show the officer how good you are,' insisted the man, with a subtle wink in her direction.

So Holly made herself cry as convincingly as she could.

'Yes, well. That's very good,' said Hughes.

'Thank you,' said Holly, smiling.

'You a-see,' said the strange man. 'She was still in a-character when you met her. Poison blood, very good, Tallulah. Such improvisation. Such a talent.'

Another policeman whispered something in the sergeant's ear and he said, 'Sir, the divers are ready. Should we send them in?'

'Divers?' said the man in the wide-brimmed hat. 'Oh, ha ha,' he laughed. 'I am so sorry, officers, there is no need for your . . . as you call them, a-divers.'

'You mean that creature had something to do with you?' said the detective inspector.

'Oh yes. We are a-making a film. A very important film. A film about people and emotions and struggle and love. It is called *The Big Scary Beast and the Poor Little Orphan*. Working title, of course. You've met the orphan, Miss Manderville. And you have obviously a-seen the big scary beast.'

The policeman eyed him suspiciously. 'Where are the cameras, then?'

'All over there,' said the man. 'All on the other side of the river and I am furious with them all.' He looked across the river, where crowds of people had gathered, and shouted, 'Furious! You hear that, Matteo?' Speaking again to the policeman he said,

'It's going to set us back days.' Then he shouted again, 'Matteo, you are a nincompoop! I said do not start the creature up until my a-say so.' 'So that creature was . . .'

'A model, yes. That's right. Magnificent, isn't she? Built entirely from a-plasticine. Isn't it amazing what they can do these days?'

`'But how come we didn't know about it? Have you got a permit to film?'

'A permit? Yes, of course we have a permit. My assistant Matteo has it. I will make him fax it to you first thing tomorrow morning then I will fire the fool.'

'Now, sir, you've cost us a lot of wasted time, not to mention terrifying half the local residents.'

The man turned to address the people on the other side of the bank and yelled, 'You hear that, Matteo, you idiot? You'll be making catfood commercials for the rest of your short career!'

'Right, I see. Well, Mr . . . er . . .'

'Firenze. Alfonso Firenze! Are you sure you have not a-heard of me? I am very a-talented.'

'Er, I don't know. Did you do that one with the giant centipede?'

'Giant Centipede? How dare you, that was Alfredo

Fintenze. I would never stoop to such low-budget tat. Centipede . . . pah!'

'OK, come on, sergeant,' said Detective Inspector Hughes. 'Let's go. False alarm.'

'What about the divers, sir?' asked the sergeant.

'Never mind that. We better go and dispel the panic, explain to everyone it was just a movie prop. Just as I suspected.'

'Right, sir,' replied the sergeant, and then shouted, 'Everyone out. False alarm.'

Detective Inspector Hughes bowed and said, 'It's a pleasure to have met you, Miss Manderville.' He shook the hand of the man in the wide-brimmed hat and said, 'I look forward to the movie, sir. *The Big Scary Beast and the* . . . er . . .'

'*The Poor Little Orphan*, yes. Just a working title. A-thank you! A-thank you. So sorry for the inconvenience. So sorry,' said the man, and the policemen got back into their cars and drove away, leaving Holly and the man alone.

'Who are you?' she said.

'My name's Ladbroke Blake,' he said in a low gravelly voice. 'I was hired by your mother to follow you.'

'My dad's wife,' corrected Holly. 'Are you going to tell her about all this?'

'You think she'd believe me? No, I'll tell her something. I just haven't figured out just what yet.'

From the river came a splash and a gasp for breath. Holly looked and saw Dirk crawl on to the bank and collapse on the ground.

'Dirk!' exclaimed Holly, diving to his side.

'A dragon,' said Ladbroke, unable to hide his surprise.

'You did it, Dirk. You did it,' she said, but Dirk didn't respond. She turned to Ladbroke. 'Please, we need to get him home.'

'I'll get the car,' said the detective.

Chapter Twenty-Four

Dirk Dilly was awoken from his fitful sleep by something damp and rough rubbing itself on his face. He forced his eyes open to find a black cat with a white face and a black smudge on its nose licking him. He picked Willow off his belly and put her down.

He was in his office. His head thumped. He groaned in pain.

He crawled to the desk and looked at the piles of newspapers there. He picked up one and read.

MOVIE MONSTER WREAKS HAVOC

In scenes that could have come straight from the latest Hollywood blockbuster, terrified East London residents thought a gigantic sea monster had emerged from the River Thames last night. The local constabulary were called and even shot at the monster before it was revealed that it was nothing more than a movie model that had got out of control. Detective Inspector Jack Hughes, one of the first to arrive on the scene said, 'The local residents were panicking, but as soon as I got a good look at it I could tell that it was in fact a mechanical device. When you've worked on the force as long as I have there's not much that you haven't seen. There was never any doubt in my mind that this was some sort of stunt gone wrong.'

Dirk picked up another and read:

MISSING CATS FOUND

The mystery of the missing cats that has been perplexing the police over the last few weeks was finally solved when local allotment owner Len Cooper discovered hundreds of cats on a disused cargo boat on the north bank of the River Thames while looking for vegetables that had been stolen from his allotment. 'I've heard of Puss in Boots,' Mr Cooper told us, 'but this was a case of Puss in Boats.'

Then he read another:

CATNAPPERS CAUGHT

Following an anonymous tip-off, the police have finally caught the perpetrators of the mysterious catnapping crimes. Mr Arthur Holt and Mr Reginald Norman are currently being held in custody. Although both men deny any involvement, forensic tests showed that the cats had all been transported in the back of a van registered in Mr Holt's name, while Mr Norman's fingerprints identified him as the driver of the van.

The two men's motives are so far unknown although Mr Holt's lawyer has released this statement: 'Arthur Holt denies any charges of cat theft levelled against him as he has long since suffered from a condition known as felinophobia, a fear of cats and all things catlike, which he contracted while holidaying on the Isle of Man.' Mr Norman's lawyer issued the statement: 'Reg says he didn't know nothing about no cats.'

Dirk put down the papers and peeked through the blinds at the street below. Across the road, leaning on a lamp-post, was the man in the wide-brimmed hat. Ladbroke Blake. But if he was still following Holly then where was she?

'Mister Dilly?' called the familiar voice of Mrs Klingerflim, knocking on the door. 'Your niece is here. She's bringing you some of my home-made medicine.'

'Thanks, Mrs K,' said Holly, entering the room, holding a brown bottle.

Dirk looked at her and smiled. 'I'm not drinking that stuff again,' he said. 'It tastes worse than Amphiptere blood.'

'Dirk!' she exclaimed. 'You're better.' She ran across the room and threw her arms round his neck.

Dirk returned the hug, then got embarrassed and said, 'All right, let's not get all sentimental. You're still being followed, you know.'

'Ladbroke? Yes, he gave me a lift. It's quite handy being followed by somebody with a car. He gets to keep a close eye on me and I get a lift from someone who can actually see the road.'

'How long have I been out?' he asked.

'A whole week this time. I've been so worried. I'm glad you're OK. They found the rest of the cats.'

'Yes, I just read that,' said Dirk. 'Mandy must have been sneaking them across the river when the Kinghorns weren't looking.'

'So what was she eating?'

'My guess is that she could reach far enough to pinch vegetables from the allotments on the other side.'

'Then her blood hadn't turned to gas at all?'

'Exactly, otherwise when I bit into her tail I would have seen bubbles instead of liquid.'

'So what would have happened if the police had hit her?'

'Her blood would have infected the water. Bad for the fish, but it wouldn't have taken to the air as the Kinghorns planned.'

'So we didn't save London?' said Holly, trying not to sound too disappointed.

'We saved much more than that. If the police had got their hands on that Amphiptere's body, humans would finally know about dragonkind. We would stop being the thing of myths and stories and become the thing of science and exploration. They would start hunting dragons with as much vigour as they did in the Middle Ages, only this time armed with sonar, radar, guns and missiles. It would have been the beginning of the war. Together we stopped that, not to mention saving a perfectly innocent Amphiptere called Mandy.'

Dirk sent a puff of smoke into the air in the shape of an Amphiptere and they both watched it gradually lose its form and disappear into nothingness.

'So,' said Dirk, 'unconvincing film monster?'

Holly explained about her encounter with the police and Ladbroke's timely arrival and how they got Dirk back to the office in the back of Ladbroke's car.

'You mean he knows about me?' said Dirk, alarmed.

'I had no choice.'

'You think he'll say anything?'

'He's given me his word that he won't. Do you want me to bring him up here?'

'No,' said Dirk. 'I'll speak to him another time. Is he following you indefinitely?'

'It's his last day today,' said Holly.

'Great,' replied Dirk. 'Because this case isn't over yet. We didn't even get close to finding Vainclaw. Tomorrow I want to go back and check out that warehouse . . .'

'You'll have to go alone this time,' said Holly.

'What do you mean?'

'I'm being sent away,' said Holly sadly.

'Away? Where?'

'To boarding school.'

'Why?'

'Dad's big-haired wife hired the detective because she knew I was bunking off school. Ladbroke didn't tell her what I'd really been doing, but there was no getting away from the fact that I haven't been at school.'

'What kind of woman sends a private detective to follow her step-daughter?'

'She's worried that I'm a liability to dad's career. He's hoping to make the cabinet after the next election. She says she can't risk the press finding out about his wayward daughter.'

'What did your dad say?'

'Nothing,' replied Holly. 'He never says anything.'

'Will you be able to get out at all?'

'It'll be tricky. The school is really strict and has really high security. Apparently there are loads of celebrities' kids there, even the prime minister's son.'

'So, when are you going?'

'They're taking me up today. Ladbroke helped me slip away to see you. I'm not even allowed to take Willow. I was hoping you might want to look after her.'

Dirk picked up the cat and stroked her. She purred contentedly.

'No problem,' he said, looking at the brown-haired, brown-eyed girl. She seemed older than when he had seen her for the first time only a couple of weeks ago. Taller, even.

Outside, a horn beeped.

Holly said, 'I'd better go. Thanks for everything, Dirk.' She hugged him one more time and then pulled away and wiped her eyes.

'Good luck,' he said. 'Maybe it won't be so bad, this new school.'

Holly nodded. 'I'll write,' she said.

'Be careful what you put in those letters. You never know who might read them,' Dirk said. Then he added, 'Hey, kiddo, it's been good having you around.'

'We'll still be friends, won't we?'

'Friends,' replied the red-backed, green-bellied, urban-based Mountain Dragon. 'Yeah, we'll still be friends.'